# The **Clue**®
# ARMCHAIR
# DETECTIVE

# The Clue®
# ARMCHAIR
# DETECTIVE

### by Lawrence Treat
### Illustrations by George Hardie

## Ballantine Books · New York

To my wife, Rose Treat, who has worked closely
with me and has contributed so much that her
name could well be on the title page as
collaborator.

Editorial  **Amy Carroll**

Design  **Denise Brown**
**Stephanie Todd**

Illustration **Malcolm Harrison,** helped to colour the pictures
**Wendy Cutlack**, assisted

Typesetting *Rowland Phototypesetting (London) Ltd*
Lithographic Reproduction *Repro Llovett, Barcelona*

First published in Great Britain in 1983 by
Dorling Kindersley Limited, 9 Henrietta Street,
Covent Garden, London WC2E 8PS

Library of Congress Catalog Card Number: 83-90072

ISBN 0-345-31179-5

Printed in United States of America

First Edition: November 1983

10 9 8 7 6 5 4 3 2

# CONTENTS

Dear Reader,

You are cordially invited to help solve the mysterious death of Mr. Humphrey Black, found brutally murdered in his house, Tudor Close.

Mr. Black was from one of the oldest families in Abbington Frith, a small English village located near the sea. His body was discovered early one morning and up until now, the police have been unable to apprehend the culprit or culprits.

Constable Dimwiddie, of the local constabulary, does, however, have six good suspects. Though each has either been born in Abbington Frith, or lived a good part of his or her life there, there are enough unexplained circumstances in their backgrounds to make them likely suspects.

He has, in the course of his duties, constructed a file on these suspects, which takes account of all the questionable incidents involving them or people close to them. In many of the instances he has ventured an opinion as to the guilt or innocence of those concerned, but in others, he has been unable to reach a conclusion.

Constable Dimwiddie believes that by reviewing the file, the person or persons responsible for Mr. Black's death will be identified. He, therefore, requires your cooperation in helping to solve the case. To make things easy for you, he has set out his notes in chronological order, and he has included a series of questions beneath each which should give you some guidance in solving the mystery. Bear in mind, he notes, that criminology is not an exact science, so many of the incidents in this book deal with probabilities rather than certainties.

All you have to do is:

1. Get hold of a pencil and some paper.

2. Read each story in the file, and study the accompanying illustration(s).

3. Before answering the questions, read them all through first, in order to get the gist of the problem. Then answer each question, one at a time and in order. Try and support your answer if you can taking account of any clues.

4. At the end of the questions, you will find the page number of the answers. If you are a beginner at solving mysteries, you may want to check your answers as you go along. If you consider yourself more of an expert, you can check them once you've finished all of them.

5. You have an extra chance to get the final solution correct. All will be revealed once you read the last answer. If you've solved the mystery correctly, give yourself a pat on the back. If not, resolve to do better next time. Then move on to the next case.

Good Luck!

# THE FILE ON THE CLUE® CHARACTERS

**PROF. PLUM**

**REV. GREEN**

### Albert Plum
Widower, former Professor of Moral and Practical Science at Wentbridge University. Born in Abbington Frith and friend since boyhood of Ivor Mustard. Recently bereaved. Formerly married to Eudocia Plum; has three children. Is devoted to children and dogs but wasn't to wife. Rumoured to be about to marry mistress, Daphne Woodcock, once formalities have been observed.

### Horatio Green
Known as Reverend but of no recognized denomination. Usually sports clerical dress. Born in Abbington Frith. Married Vanessa Simpkins, a friend of his mother. Left village when wife died under suspicious circumstances but returned some years ago bearing above title. Unmarried at present but known to be fond of women.
Keen photographer.

### Cynthia Scarlet
Single, former "Artiste of the Air" in Jake Jasper's Travelling Circus. Arrived in Abbington Frith one Spring bank holiday. After death of circus owner, Simon McNiff, became engaged to Sir Montague Black of Tudor Close. Upon Sir Montague's untimely demise she was the constant companion of Mr. Humphrey Black, his brother. Fond of chocolate eclairs and expensive jewellery.

**MISS SCARLET**

**MRS. PEACOCK**

### Penelope Peacock
Widow, former wife of Lieutenant Percy Peacock of H.M.S. Insensible, and sister of Albert Plum. One of the last Abbington Frith Peacocks. Of indeterminate age but definitely not young. Lives alone but has relatives abroad. Keen butterfly collector.

### Ivor Mustard
Nickname "Colonel". Born in Abbington Frith and married to local girl, Abigail Mustard, nanny, for many years. No children. Started out as actor but rapidly discovered he had no future there. Good sportsman and member of all Abbington Frith's clubs. Now owns and works at village pub – The Perfect Ace. Smokes pipe.

### Beryl White
Née Smythe, Husband Henry reported "missing presumed dead" after last war. Grew up on Tudor Close estate but worked as maid and housekeeper before returning to big house as cook. Reputed to be one of the best cooks in England, she is now retired but, on special occasions, works at Tudor Close.

**COL. MUSTARD**

**MRS. WHITE**

# THE VANDALS

When Professor Plum was young and poor, he worked for a time as history master at Abbington Frith's prestigious Rondo Academy. There, his students in their infinite wisdom, nicknamed him *Old Witless*. Professor Plum had trouble with his nickname and with his pupils; to him they were nine-year-old scalawags who didn't want to learn, and kept asking how you could make money out of history. This question was unanswerable until Plum came up with an idea. Each of the students was to put two pence a week into a fund, and he'd match the total at the end of the term. The class could then stage a realistic Battle of Hastings, followed by a picnic.

The idea worked and the money was kept in a cash box locked in the desk drawer. By the end of term it came to five pounds. On the morning of the picnic, Professor Plum walked into his classroom and found it as illustrated. He knew that any one of his scalawags could have sneaked in during the night and wrecked the classroom, but he singled out three as the most likely suspects. These were Hugo Furst, Peter Peacock III, and little Johnny White. Professor Plum insisted that the three turn out their pockets, the contents of which are shown here: (top) Hugo Furst, (middle) Peter Peacock III, (bottom) little Johnny White.

Who was guilty, and why?

**1.** *Had the money been stolen?* Yes ☐ No ☐

**2.** *Do you think that the scalawags wanted to sabotage the picnic?* Yes ☐ No ☐

**3.** *Was the damage likely to have been caused by more than one boy?* Yes ☐ No ☐

**4.** *Is there anything in sight that has been left undisturbed?* Yes ☐ No ☐

**5.** *Was the screwdriver used to force open the desk drawer?* Yes ☐ No ☐

**6.** *How do you think the cash box was opened?* Key ☐ Screwdriver ☐ Other ☐

**7.** *Did any of the boys have incriminating objects in his pocket?* Yes ☐ No ☐

**8.** *Who has the strongest motive for stealing the money?*

**9.** *Who stole the money?*

ANSWERS PAGE 58

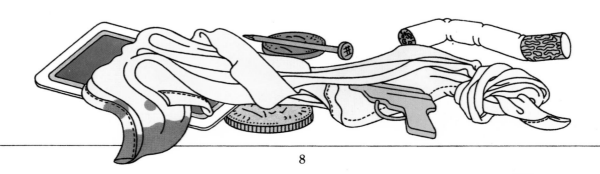

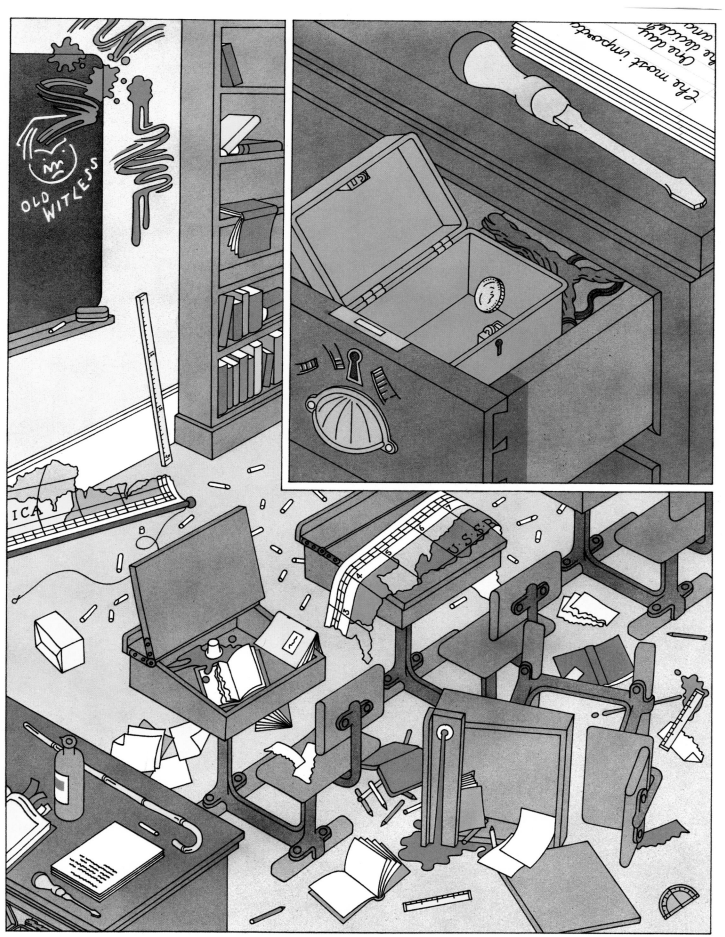

# AT THE BOATHOUSE

Long before she became the dowager dame of Abbington Frith, Penelope Peacock (née just plain Plum) had led a more frivolous life. Every day she laved, bathed, powdered and primped, and the product was pleasing to many, including the dashing young lieutenant of H.M.S. Insensible. To her subsequent regret, she married him. The regret came about because Lieutenant Percy Peacock did a little too much dashing.

His conquests were a scandal to the villagers, but they watched with considerable interest when the lieutenant eyed the lovely Mercedes Diesel, for she happened to be the fiancée of Penelope's brother Wilmot. The rivalry between Wilmot and the lieutenant was fanned to a white heat when the village selected them as opposing captains in the annual tug-of-war at the summer fête.

Just before tea-time a few days before the contest, young Wilmot and the lieutenant came to the boathouse to choose their teams. They arrived promptly, but presently Wilmot rushed out of the door of the boathouse and into the midst of a croquet game. He shouted for help and said, "There's been an accident – the lieutenant fell and hurt himself!"

Players and spectators rushed over and found the lieutenant lying in front of the fireplace. He was dead. Constable Dimwiddie marked the outline of the body and noted the bloody area on the base of the fireplace set where, Wilmot said|Percy had suffered his fatal wound.

Wilmot, the chief suspect, kept saying that it had all been an accident. Lieutenant Peacock, he claimed, was testing the strength of the rope when it broke, causing him to trip over a chair and fall, striking his head.

"It's obvious," Wilmot said, "that if I had hit him with the base of the fireplace set, as some of you seem to believe, the contact would have been at the edge or

10

underside, but never on the upper surface. That could happen only if he fell, as he did."

Two days after the incident, the crime laboratory confirmed that the fire tools were clean and that microscopic bits of metal from the wound matched the metal composition of the upper surface of the fireplace set. Nowhere else could they find either blood or metallic fragments. If you had been investigating the case, would you have exonerated Wilmot?

**1.** *Is Wilmot's story credible?* Yes □ No □

**2.** *Are the rope and overturned chair strongly supportive of Wilmot's account?* Yes □ No □

**3.** *Is there any evidence to support Wilmot's statement that he rushed out immediately after Percy's fall?* Yes □ No □

**4.** *Was the probable purpose of the fire to heat the room?* Yes □ No □

**5.** *Is there evidence of a disagreement or fight between Wilmot and Lieutenant Peacock?* Yes □ No □

**6.** *Did Wilmot hit the lieutenant over the head with a croquet mallet?* Yes □ No □

**7.** *Did Wilmot hit Lieutenant Peacock over the head with the base of the fire set?* Yes □ No □

**8.** *Could Wilmot have scraped blood from Lieutenant Peacock's wound and smeared it on the base of the fire set?* Yes □ No □

**9.** *Do you think Wilmot sneaked out of the front of the boathouse and then disposed of a possible weapon?* Yes □ No □

**10.** *Is there any evidence of someone having stepped to the edge of the lake?* Yes □ No □

**11.** *Do you think Wilmot killed Lieutenant Peacock?* Yes □ No □ *If so, with what?* ANSWERS PAGE 58

# WITCHCRAFT

C. Atterbury Penn, the drama critic called "Poison Penn" by his colleagues, delighted in the phrase that destroyed, and the word that demolished. His enemies were everybody who'd ever written a play or appeared on the stage, amateur or professional. His friends had yet to be born, but what counted most was the public. They read his *Poison Penn* reviews, delighted in his malice and followed his advice. He determined the plays that were flops or sold to overflow audiences, the actors who were made or made destitute. He was paid whether the play was a success or not, and thus got the best out of his own reviews.

The small fortune that he earned doing others out of theirs he invested in pursuing his real interest – black magic. He had bought a splendid house on the outskirts of Abbington Frith, and furnished it with an incredible array of voodoo and similar paraphernalia. This made him a scandal to the entire village. Since nobody could stand him he lived by himself.

On the night of October 31st he was alone as usual and was working on his latest cuttings when his neighbours heard shots, followed by a series of unearthly shrieks. Trembling, apprehensive, each of them afraid to approach the Penn house alone, they waited at the bottom of the drive until a crowd of them had gathered before they dared investigate. What you see now is what they saw. Afraid to go near the fallen Penn, they summoned Doctor Brunhilder. Not finding any evidence of foul play, he pronounced Penn dead of heart failure. He was certain of this diagnosis because everyone knew Penn had recently been hospitalized for a heart condition.

Had you been present, would you have agreed with the diagnosis?

**1.** *Was this a special night?* Yes ☐ No ☐

**2.** *Was it likely that Penn was superstitious?* Yes ☐ No ☐

**3.** *Do you think that several people had visited Penn on this fatal evening?* Yes ☐ No ☐

**4.** *Were any of them witches, or pseudo-witches?* Yes ☐ No ☐

**5.** *Do you think that the objects on the stairs belonged to Penn?* Yes ☐ No ☐

**6.** *Do you think that the objects on the stairs belonged to children?* Yes ☐ No ☐

**7.** *Was there anything present to account for the "shots"?* Yes ☐ No ☐

**8.** *Do you think that Penn underwent a severe fright?* Yes ☐ No ☐

**9.** *Was the cause of Penn's death natural?* Yes ☐ No ☐

**10.** *Do you think Penn's death was an accident?* Yes ☐ No ☐

**11.** *Would you arrest and interrogate anyone?* Yes ☐ No ☐

ANSWERS PAGES 58

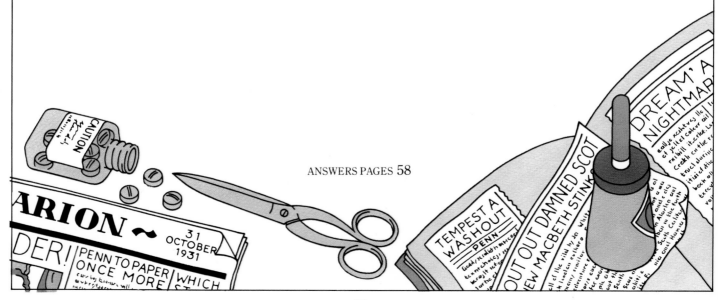

# THE DEATH OF BILLIKINS

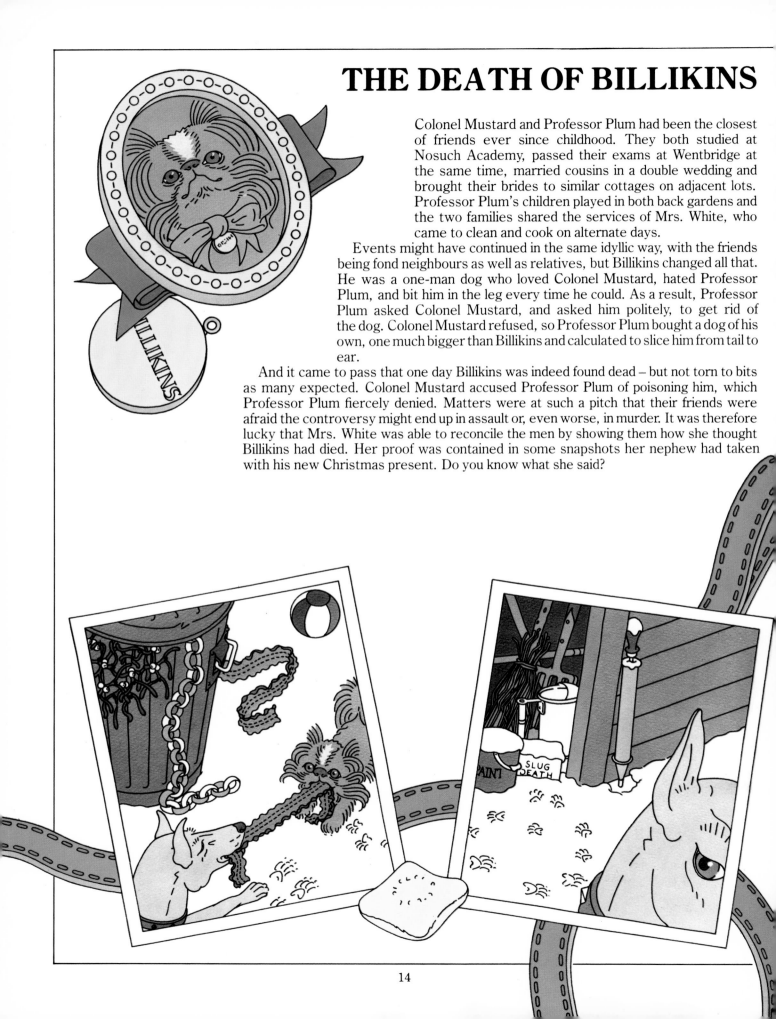

Colonel Mustard and Professor Plum had been the closest of friends ever since childhood. They both studied at Nosuch Academy, passed their exams at Wentbridge at the same time, married cousins in a double wedding and brought their brides to similar cottages on adjacent lots. Professor Plum's children played in both back gardens and the two families shared the services of Mrs. White, who came to clean and cook on alternate days.

Events might have continued in the same idyllic way, with the friends being fond neighbours as well as relatives, but Billikins changed all that. He was a one-man dog who loved Colonel Mustard, hated Professor Plum, and bit him in the leg every time he could. As a result, Professor Plum asked Colonel Mustard, and asked him politely, to get rid of the dog. Colonel Mustard refused, so Professor Plum bought a dog of his own, one much bigger than Billikins and calculated to slice him from tail to ear.

And it came to pass that one day Billikins was indeed found dead – but not torn to bits as many expected. Colonel Mustard accused Professor Plum of poisoning him, which Professor Plum fiercely denied. Matters were at such a pitch that their friends were afraid the controversy might end up in assault or, even worse, in murder. It was therefore lucky that Mrs. White was able to reconcile the men by showing them how she thought Billikins had died. Her proof was contained in some snapshots her nephew had taken with his new Christmas present. Do you know what she said?

1. *Were the dogs well loved?*  Yes ☐ No ☐

2. *Did the dogs like each other?*  Yes ☐ No ☐

3. *Did both dogs drink from the same bowl?*  Yes ☐ No ☐

4. *Were there other things to eat?*  Yes ☐ No ☐

5. *Do you see any garden poisons in the photos?*
*Yes* ☐ *No* ☐

6. *Do you think that Billikins ate any of them?*
*Yes* ☐ *No* ☐

7. *Do you see anything else that might be poisonous?*
*Yes* ☐ *No* ☐

8. *How did Billikins die?*

ANSWERS PAGE 58

# NOT A PRETTY SIGHT

Reverend Horatio Green, in his youth, was something of a sissy. He was neat and tidy, dressed in co-ordinating clothes, ate up all his food without leaving any crumbs, read the Bible for fun, and paid careful attention to everything his mother said. Consequently, when she advised him to marry Vanessa Simpkins, the elder daughter of her oldest friend, he said "yes" without hesitation.

Vanessa and Horatio were the subjects of a lively debate among their friends and acquaintances. There were those who said that, while Horatio had some good points, the best of them was Vanessa. Others defended Horatio and said that, although he'd always liked stupid women, he'd gone too far with Vanessa. As for those who liked both Horace and Vanessa, there were none.

Regardless of which side of the controversy you might like to take, it ended as a practical matter at about 2:45 p.m. on a lovely July afternoon, according to Constable Dimwiddie's account. Horatio had gone out in his punt on the lake and returned at about 4:00 p.m. to find Vanessa dead and the Constable waiting for him. His shock was about what one might expect, and in answering the questions Dimwiddie put to him he made the following statements.

Which of them do you think are true, false, or impossible to prove?

**1.** *"We brought a picnic lunch to the lakeside."*
*True* ☐ *False* ☐ *Impossible to prove* ☐

**2.** *"We played tic-tac-toe for a while."*
*True* ☐ *False* ☐ *Impossible to prove* ☐

**3.** *"We drank a little wine." True* ☐
*False* ☐ *Impossible to prove* ☐

**4.** *"We ate up all the food except some sandwiches."*
*True* ☐ *False* ☐ *Impossible to prove* ☐

**5.** *"The last time I saw Vanessa she was asleep."*
*True* ☐ *False* ☐ *Impossible to prove* ☐

**6.** *"I left her to go punting." True* ☐
*False* ☐ *Impossible to prove* ☐

**7.** *"We were completely compatible." True* ☐ *False* ☐
*Impossible to prove* ☐

**8.** *"I had no possible reason for harming her."*
*True* ☐ *False* ☐ *Impossible to prove* ☐

**9.** *"She had £200 in her purse." True* ☐ *False* ☐
*Impossible to prove* ☐

**10.** *"She had brought her fur coat along." True* ☐
*False* ☐ *Impossible to prove* ☐

**11.** *"It's obvious that whoever killed her, must have done it to steal her things." True* ☐ *False* ☐
*Impossible to prove* ☐

**12.** *"It certainly wasn't me who killed her." True* ☐
*False* ☐ *Impossible to prove* ☐

ANSWERS PAGE 58

# LOVERS' LEAP

Anybody who keeps five thousand pounds overnight under his bed deserves to lose it, and Dr. Brunhilder, who had it and then lost it, agreed. Still, he was unworried. How far can a butler and a green-eyed parlour maid get with five thousand pounds in large notes?

After several days, however, and the only lead a reported sighting of the lovers leaving the railway station, Dr. Brunhilder and Constable Dimwiddie were certain that the lovers were in hiding. The police, however, persevered and came up with a lead. A Nicaraguan freighter was due in the nearby port and they believed Homer would try to get on it, but they also believed that Mrs. White, the butler's sister, would help them. Since she was the best cook in Abbington Frith, and maybe in the whole of England, and since Dr. Brunhilder cared more for his stomach than his bank account, and certainly more than for his patients, he did nothing that might make trouble for her.

The constable and Dr. Brunhilder were right about one thing – Mrs. White did indeed tell the couple that the police were on their trail and that they'd better put the money in a safe place, because if they were caught with the money in their possession, the evidence against them would be overwhelming. They were doomed, and they knew it. But even before the ship docked, Homer's whereabouts became known. Young Anthony Bright, cub reporter on the Abbington Frith Gazette, came upon this scene while out covering local beauty spots. The sight of the pretty young girl dressed in her best clothes with a bullet in her head sent him running for Constable Dimwiddie, but not before he stopped to cover the body.

Constable Dimwiddie examined the revolver and ascertained that two shots had been fired from it. He also studied the bank notes and an envelope, addressed to him, which contained the following note:

*"I know that you are on my trail and that I have only a few more days of freedom. I was never made for a life behind bars. I was made for action and adventure. My butlering was all a mistake and I refuse to return to it. There is only one solution, and I take my green-eyed darling with me. As for money – what good is it? I toss it to the waves.*

*"I have only one regret. I'm sorry I took the doctor's shoes. They don't fit and they gave me blisters, so I return them willingly.*

*Homer B. Smythe"*

The constable and the reporter put their heads together, but unfortunately their conclusions were wide apart. It remains for you to solve the puzzle.

May success be yours!

**1.** *Does the note suggest a suicide pact?* Yes ☐ No ☐

**2.** *Do you think the parlour maid expected to die?*
Yes ☐ No ☐

**3.** *Did she struggle?* Yes ☐ No ☐

**4.** *Did Homer toss all of the money away?* Yes ☐ No ☐

**5.** *Could he have kept some back in a hiding place?*
Yes ☐ No ☐

**6.** *Did Homer shoot himself?* Yes ☐ No ☐

**7.** *Did he break the fence while trying to throw himself over the cliff?* Yes ☐ No ☐

**8.** *Could he have left another way?* Yes ☐ No ☐

**9.** *Did Homer fake the incident to cover his tracks?*
Yes ☐ No ☐

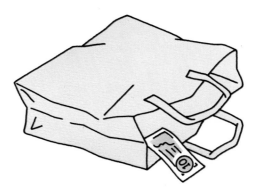

ANSWERS PAGE 58

# ALL IN GOOD FUN

The Robin Hood Club met four times a year, in the dark of the moon and in a pitch black room, so that no one knew for certain who the other members were. It had been formed to right the wrongs of society through the commission of what the members called "good deeds" and what their detractors said were pranks, or simply practical jokes. Though people were divided as to whether they did any real good, it was generally believed they meant no real harm.

At the first meeting of every year, four projects were decided on, each to be carried out three months apart. They ranged from letting down the tyres of Anthony B. Mockery's Jaguar, whose driving was a menace to the entire village, especially old ladies and children, to supplying a new set of false teeth to One-Eye Mulligan, who had had his run over.

It was only natural that eventually the club would decide to take care of Henry Ecclestrip, the banker with a list of enemies more or less duplicating the official census. Ecclestrip delighted in charging high interest and in foreclosing mortgages. He liked to think of himself as the banker who always said "No". His only pleasure in life was to be found round the billiard table. In his capacity as financial advisor to Sir Montague Black, he had persuaded him to let Tudor Close's billiard room become his own private preserve. No one entered without an invitation, not even Sir Montague.

And, it was there, one April Fool's Day, that Constable Dimwiddie was called in to investigate the death of Ecclestrip, who had apparently slipped on a banana peel and cracked his head in the resulting fall.

In view of the circumstances, the Constable was convinced from the start that this was the work of the Robin Hood Club, whose procedure was secret and rigid but well known to himself. Each member had a number. When a project was decided upon, the numbers were put into a hat and the member whose number was chosen first was in charge of the project. He not only had to undertake the commission, but had to leave some form of identification to show that he had indeed taken care of the business.

Dimwiddie reasoned rightly that counting up the number of pranks would lead him to the culprit. Once he had this number, he could then call upon the proper authorities to obtain the name of the corresponding member.

Can you list the pranks and thus decide who's number came up?

ANSWERS PAGE 59

# UNDER THE BIG TOP

An annual attraction in Abbington Frith was the Spring bank holiday visit by Jake Jasper's Travelling Circus. Every May, their big tent was set up on the village green and for three days the villagers were thrilled and amazed.

Although the fat woman was weighed carefully every day and the talking horses performed in three languages, including Latin, the rest of the company were no linguists. They were neither expert nor extraordinary. In fact, they were simply exes. Jake, the tiger tamer, was more renowned for the fact that he had had one leg bitten off by a beast, than for making animals behave; Ethel, the "Equestrian Enchantress", had a morbid fear of heights and clung desperately to her mounts; Sandy, the "Candystripe Clown", always looked so glum that nobody laughed, and Johannes the German juggler stood rooted to the spot, having broken his foot with a dropped medicine club.

As a result, the circus was continually losing money. In fact, this year Simon McNiff, it's child-and-animal-hating hotdog vendor, had collected enough mortgages on the circus to become its owner.

He was the opposite of Jake. When McNiff took over the role of ringmaster, he cut everyone's salary by 10% to pay for his own, ordered everyone to call him "Sir", and took to strutting around in his top hat, cutaway, swagger stick and cigar. He even instituted a nightly snoop around the circus to make certain that both the animals and performers were in bed and safely asleep by 9 o'clock.

The circus folk might conceivably have stood this if it hadn't been for Cynthia Scarlet. Cynthia, the "Artiste of the Air", was as beautiful as she was near-sighted, and seemingly virtuous to a fault. It was inevitable that, after she had twice rebuffed McNiff, she had some third thoughts. With a tear in her eye, for the sake of form, of course, she acceded.

She should not have. Although she never divulged exactly what had happened, it was clear to everyone that Cynthia had to be avenged. The vengeance was wreaked according to the best traditions, in the dark of the moon and in the middle of the night. The tiger was the only witness and he refused to talk.

Constable Dimwiddie had been flitting around the neighbourhood searching out the night-flying death's head hawk moth *(Acherontia atropos)* when he heard a shot and went off to investigate. Switching on the central spotlight, he saw this.

From the very beginning, he found the most baffling element of the crime was was the path of the fatal bullet. He couldn't figure out how it could have travelled directly downward, through the top of McNiff's head, down the length of his torso and out through his heel. All the performers had the same alibi – they were fast asleep and only woke up when they heard a shot.

Can you decide who lied, and who fired the fatal shot?

**1.** *Had the ground been swept after last night's performance?* Yes ☐ No ☐

**2.** *Are the footsteps McNiff's?* Yes ☐ No ☐

**3.** *Was McNiff hard to spot in the dark?* Yes ☐ No ☐

**4.** *Do you think that he saw his assailant?* Yes ☐ No ☐

**5.** *Do you think the shot was fired from the aerialist's perch?* Yes ☐ No ☐

**6.** *Do you think the shot was fired from the trapeze?* Yes ☐ No ☐

**7.** *Do you think the shot was fired from horseback?* Yes ☐ No ☐

**8.** *Who shot McNiff and how was it done?*

ANSWERS PAGE 59

# TENNIS, ANYONE?

On one brutally hot day Caspar Willoughby lost the Abbington Frith championship to Ivor Mustard in straight sets, and the Exeter twins (Nigel and Neville) were not the only ones who thought that Caspar had thrown the game. Since a lot of money changed hands, there were ample reasons to explain why, shortly after the finish, it became obvious that Caspar had played his last tennis.

Horatio Green had witnessed the murder while out taking photographs. "I couldn't tell which twin it was," he said, "not from the distance where I was. But Caspar was walking past the clubhouse porch when Nigel or Neville, it was one or the other, stopped him. The two had an argument and I could see they were both angry. Caspar finally gave the twin a shove and then started to walk off. The moment his back was turned, either Nigel or Neville picked up a rock from the path and gave him a great forearm swipe on the side of the head. He fell like a ball boy with heatstroke. The twin bent over him and shrugged and then ran off into the clubhouse. Next thing I knew, both twins came out and sat down with drinks (one with a Bloody Mary – symbolic, what?). Then I called the police. Anybody who hits a man from behind is an absolute cad and should never had been admitted to the club!"

After examining the body, Constable Dimwiddie proceeded immediately to the porch and questioned the twins. Nigel, at the left, said, "The last time I saw Caspar was when the match ended. After it was over, Neville and I ordered a drink at the bar and brought our glasses out here, where we sat down to relax. What's this all about?"

Neville, at the right, said, "The last time I saw Caspar was when the match ended. After it was over, Nigel and I ordered a drink at the bar and brought our glasses out here, where we sat down to relax. What's this all about?"

Constable Dimwiddie listened politely, and later returned to have them sign their typed statements. In another few minutes he asked one twin to come along to the station. If you had been Constable Dimwiddie whom would you have arrested?

**1.** *Were the Exeter twins identical?* Yes ☐ No ☐

**2.** *Could the twins see the body from where they sat?* Yes ☐ No ☐

**3.** *Did one of the twins tell the truth?* Yes ☐ No ☐

**4.** *Do you think they discussed their denials of the crime beforehand?* Yes ☐ No ☐

**5.** *Was there any evidence that either of the twins had committed an act of violence?* Yes ☐ No ☐

**6.** *Was the crime premeditated?* Yes ☐ No ☐

**7.** *Who killed Caspar?* Nigel ☐ Neville ☐

ANSWERS PAGE 59

# PEACOCK'S POSER

Regularly every morning Jenny Goodheart got up at five, mounted her bicycle, picked up her batch of morning papers and made her deliveries.

One of her stops was at Winston Peacock's. He lived alone and was reputed to have a fortune tucked away somewhere in his house, which was built into a hill so that the only access was the front door and a couple of side windows. Usually Winston waved to Jenny, and as she pedalled off she could hear the bolt of the door being pulled back.

On the last day of the year he greeted her as usual, but the next morning, when there was no sign of him, she assumed that he had the same hangover as most of her customers. On January 2nd, however, there was a paper and two milk bottles still lying in front of his door. Alarmed, she dismounted from her bicycle and peeked through the nearest window. Though none of the lights were on, she could see Winston, apparently dead, lying on the floor near his desk. The sight set her trembling, and she got on her bicycle and rode as fast as she could to the village police station.

Constable Dimwiddie went straight to the house. There, after verifying Jenny's account as well as he could through a window, he called his colleagues. They had to smash the window in order to gain entrance. Inside, they saw what you see, and knew immediately what had happened.

"He shot himself," they said, one after the other. "Suicide."

But Dimwiddie was smart enough not to make a quick decision, and he reserved judgment until he'd examined the house more thoroughly. After fiddling around with the bolt, he made his decision.

What was it?

**1.** *When did Winston Peacock die? New Year's Eve* ☐ *New Year's Day* ☐ *New Year's night* ☐

**2.** *Was the door securely bolted? Yes* ☐ *No* ☐

**3.** *Could the door be opened without unbolting it?* *Yes* ☐ *No* ☐

**4.** *Would the bar of the latch automatically fall into its notch when the door was closed? Yes* ☐ *No* ☐

**5.** *Did anyone search for money? Yes* ☐ *No* ☐

**6.** *Are there good reasons for the suicide theory?* *Yes* ☐ *No* ☐

**7.** *Had he been cooking? Yes* ☐ *No* ☐

**8.** *Had the rug been carefully rolled back?* *Yes* ☐ *No* ☐

**9.** *Are there good reasons for discounting the suicide theory? Yes* ☐ *No* ☐

**10.** *Would Winston's heirs have a motive for killing him?* *Yes* ☐ *No* ☐

**11.** *If you think he was murdered, give your explanation of how the murderer bolted the door upon leaving.*

ANSWERS PAGE 59

26

# TRIAL RUN

The Abbington Frith cat burglar was unquestionably the greatest jewel thief of his generation. Constable Dimwiddie had no proof of his identity, though he strongly suspected he was one of his favourite three suspects – Plum, Mustard and Green – but he did know the thief was superstitious and a man of habit. He always robbed on the last quarter of the moon, give or take a day or so. It was his lucky period.

The thief always planned his getaway with great care, and he usually learnt the best route from a cook, a housemaid or a nurse, for his charm was irresistible.

He had had several close encounters, but Constable Dimwiddie hoped the last one would be at the engagement ball of Sir Montague Black and Cynthia Scarlet. With a fair representation of the important jewellery of the entire county due for display on ear, wrist, bosom and neck, the cat burglar was certain to be present. Dimwiddie was going to be ready, he had devised a plan.

On the night before the ball, the thief made a trial run of his escape route. He did it hand in hand with Ruby, the unsylph-like kitchen maid whom he had charmed into guiding him. She led him down a back staircase, through a store room and along the length of a narrow corridor that brought them to the small, trysting room adjacent to the ballroom. Beyond, she explained, there was a garden with a low wall that he could easily climb. On the other side of it would be his car.

The thief squeezed Ruby's little hand and put his arm halfway round her waist, thanked her, and together they retraced their steps.

On the night of the ball a host of jewels were on display. But to Dimwiddie's surprise and chagrin, nothing was stolen.

Why?

**1.** *Do you think a hidden camera was placed somewhere in the room?*  Yes ☐ No ☐

**2.** *Could the doors have been locked?*  Yes ☐ No ☐

**3.** *If locked, would there have been any problems in opening them?*  Yes ☐ No ☐

**4.** *Did Ruby apparently lie about the height of the garden wall?*  Yes ☐ No ☐

**5.** *What did the thief see that made him an honest man the next night?*

ANSWERS PAGE 59

# IN THE ACT

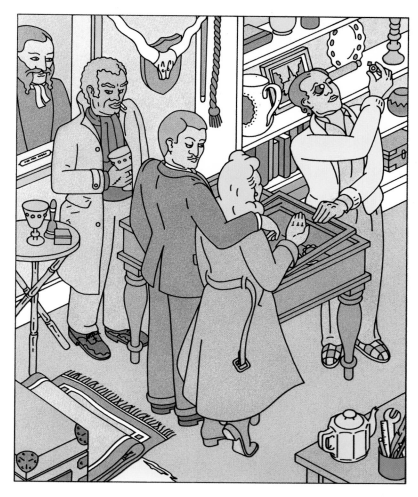

This is the scene as reconstructed later on when the man at the left blatantly stole several valuable items while Sir Montague Black and his fiancée Cynthia Scarlet were selecting her ring on the day of their engagement ball. The store, I. Cheet, Antiques, was insured for the full amount of the items.

Sir Montague and Cynthia had spent several hours choosing the biggest, most expensive ring she could find. She had an inkling their engagement might not last, and she wanted some insurance against their breaking up. As it turned out, this was a good policy.

How would you go about apprehending the thief, whom you see in the act of stealing in the sketch?

**1.** *Do you think Cynthia was aware of the theft?*
*Yes ☐ No ☐*

**2.** *Do you think Sir Montague was aware of the theft?*
*Yes ☐ No ☐*

**3.** *Do you think the clerk was aware of the theft?*
*Yes ☐ No ☐*

**4.** *Do you think that the thief was a professional?*
*Yes ☐ No ☐*

**5.** *Do you think that the theft was well planned?*
*Yes ☐ No ☐*

**6.** *Did he leave any clues as to his whereabouts?*
*Yes ☐ No ☐*

ANSWERS PAGE 56

# APHRODITE'S REVENGE

Mr. Black inherited both Tudor Close and the willowy Miss Scarlet from his elder brother, Sir Montague Black. On the night that Mr. Black gained his inheritance and Sir Montague lost his life, eight of the bedrooms in Tudor Close were unoccupied. The local physician, Dr. Brunhilder, placed the great event at about three a.m. on that moonless night, and the cause as a less than loving encounter with the goddess Aphrodite.

Aside from the servants' quarters – and all the servants were young and innocent – four people were sleeping in the house that night, and for the other three, Sir Montague had previously made special provisions in his will. Each was to receive a generous amount of money upon Sir Montague's death. The three were:

Cynthia Scarlet, a former "aeriel artiste" who loved both Sir Montague and chocolate, though she got more satisfaction from the latter than the former;

Selwyn Black, Sir Montague's son, endowed with the thirst for two quarts of spirits a day, but lacking the purse to do much more than barely sustain it;

Stanley Zambesi, or Solly, who had come up from the mines with Sir Montague and acted as a bodyguard (Sir Montague's enemies wrote him scurrilous letters in five languages and threatened murder).

Questioned, all three said they'd heard either a crash, a thud or a shot, but no one followed it up. Cynthia said she turned over on her left side, went straight back to sleep and dreamt of chocolate eclairs, remnants of which were found in her bed. Both Selwyn and Solly claimed never to have left their beds, and each accused the other. Solly said that Selwyn had been too drunk to remember what he'd done, but that he, Solly, had heard Selwyn go downstairs and engage in some kind of argument with his father.

Accused, Selwyn laughed a silly, empty little laugh and went staggering around the room playing detective. In the course of his investigating, he lost his balance and scraped his hand against a nail on which a piece of cloth was impaled. It matched Solly's jacket which Solly claimed he hadn't worn in months.

The evidence is in front of you.

**1.** *Did Sir Montague have a reason for coming downstairs?* Yes ☐ No ☐

**2.** *Was this an "inside job"?* Yes ☐ No ☐

**3.** *Did all three suspects have a motive for murder?* Yes ☐ No ☐

**4.** *Did Aphrodite fall off her pedestal accidentally?* Yes ☐ No ☐

**5.** *Did Sir Montague probably see his assailant?* Yes ☐ No ☐

**6.** *Did Sir Montague attempt to shoot at his assailant?* Yes ☐ No ☐

**7.** *Do you think that the bottom of a door is a sensible place to put a nail?* Yes ☐ No ☐

**8.** *Was it likely that this nail tore the jacket of someone brushing up against it?* Yes ☐ No ☐

**9.** *Did the killer have a chocolate eclair?* Yes ☐ No ☐

**10.** *Had the killing been planned?* Yes ☐ No ☐

**11.** *Who killed Sir Montague Black?*

ANSWERS PAGE **60**

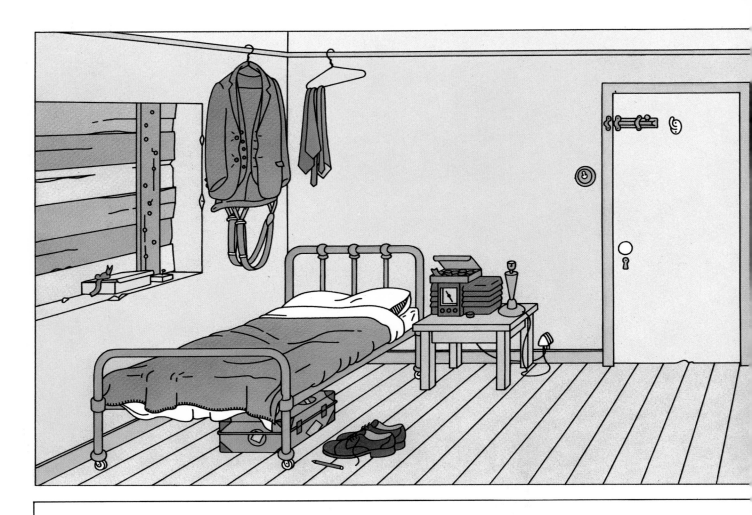

# THE KIDNAPPED KID

Rupert Plum was a sweet little boy. He brushed his teeth every night, said his prayers every morning and was at the foot of his class, but was he worth a million? His mother thought not, and when little Rupert was kidnapped and the ransom set at a cool million, she tried to bargain. The trouble was, she had no one to bargain with. The kidnapper had made his demand and set his deadline, which was at the end of a six-day period.

Professor Plum didn't like the deal. "That's no way for a kidnapper to behave," he said. "He's supposed to bargain and to phone every night, but the way he's running things, I'm supposed to raise the whole sum, and that's it. I say it's not fair."

Eudocia Plum took a different point of view. "It's not a matter of fairness or justice," she said. "It's a practical question. Do I or don't I have a spare million? I don't. Anyhow, even if I did, I'm not sure Rupert's worth it!"

Meanwhile the police went about the job of following up all the clues that were being phoned in. The tip that a man and a boy in a neighbouring town were hiding in a room in 202 Worms Street was neither the most promising lead nor an obviously false one, but when the police got there, they were told that the occupant of the third floor rear had left with a boy about twenty minutes ago. The informant hadn't seen the boy, but he'd heard him, and he hadn't seen the car they'd gone off in, but he'd heard the engine.

Constable Dimwiddie, representing the parents, had a feeling about the room from the moment he stepped into it, and on closer examination he was pretty sure he was onto something. As a result, he sent out a general alarm, with a description.

What were the details of his description, and how had he figured them out?

1. *Had the kidnapping been planned well ahead of time?*
*Yes ☐ No ☐*

2. *Could Rupert have escaped?  Yes ☐ No ☐*

3. *Did the kidnappers expect to kill Rupert?*
*Yes ☐ No ☐*

4. *Was the kidnapper short?  Yes ☐ No ☐*

5. *Was he fat?  Yes ☐ No ☐*

6. *Was he probably young (under 30)?  Yes ☐ No ☐*

7. *Was he neat?  Yes ☐ No ☐*

8. *Had he left in a hurry?  Yes ☐ No ☐*

9. *What was the colour of his hair?  Brown ☐*
*Black ☐ Red ☐ Blonde ☐*

10. *Did he have a dog?  Yes ☐ No ☐*

11. *What was Dimwiddie's main item of identification?*

12. *How many people, besides Rupert, did Dimwiddie say*
*would be found in the car?  One ☐ More than one ☐*

ANSWERS PAGE **60**

# A MATTER OF GRAVITY

Val Haller worked at the Abbington Frith Garage and was conceded to be one of the best mechanics in the county. He was accurate, fast, and never wasted time talking, but he was apparently horrified when his patched-up car rolled down the hill and struck Dr. Brunhilder's big Speedster, with results that you can see. When Constable Dimwiddie got to the scene, he found Val and Dr. Brunhilder's housekeeper, Mrs. White, discussing the catastrophe. The constable made a thorough investigation, then questioned both Val and Mrs. White, separately, of course.

Val said, "It was that brake of mine. I fixed it a week ago, but you never can tell. I just left it for a moment while I went to buy some cigarettes. I feel awful about what my car did. Lots of people like the doc and respected him, and just because I testified against him in the malpractice case didn't mean I had anything against him, the way Mrs. White certainly did.

"What did I do? When I heard the crash, I rushed out of the shop and when I didn't see the car, I ran down the hill to see what had happened. Mrs. White was already standing next to the doctor and she told me that he was dead."

Mrs. White said, "I heard the crash and rushed out. Val was already there, and I took one look at the doctor and knew he was dead. Everybody knows that ever since my brother absconded with the doctor's money, he and I didn't get along. I don't deny it, but what has that got to do with an accident?"

Constable Dimwiddie put on his best thinking cap and reviewed the statements of both Val and Mrs. White. What conclusion did he reach and what evidence did he give at the coroner's inquest?

**1.** *Did the Speedster have a flat tyre?* Yes ☐ No ☐

**2.** *Had Dr. Brunhilder been changing the tyre?* Yes ☐ No ☐

**3.** *Did he have all the necessary tools?* Yes ☐ No ☐

**4.** *Would he have heard a car rolling down the hill?* Yes ☐ No ☐

**5.** *Could the crash have knocked him over and into the brick post?* Yes ☐ No ☐

**6.** *Had someone been waiting by the brick wall?* Yes ☐ No ☐

**7.** *Had someone recently walked up the path?* Yes ☐ No ☐

**8.** *Is is possible that the doctor was killed before the crash?* Yes ☐ No ☐

**9.** *Did Val and Mrs. White both have motives for killing the doctor?* Yes ☐ No ☐

**10.** *State your conclusion, with your reasons:*

a)     *This was an accident*
b)     *Val killed the doctor*
c)     *Mrs. White killed the doctor*

ANSWERS PAGE 60

# THE PERFECT ACE

Colonel Mustard was a disappointed man. He had failed to make a living as an actor, and his one moment of glory occurred when he won the Club Championship, and then everyone had thought the match was thrown. For some years now he'd been the publican of The Perfect Ace, named in honour of his great tennis victory. A pub wasn't what he fancied for himself, but at least he hoped to make a living of sorts.

The village of Abbington Frith was not a great tourist attraction, but an occasional tourist did come and ask what there was to see, and what better place than The Perfect Ace? There, Colonel Mustard served up, as he liked to remind his customers, the best brew in the whole of England. And there, practically every day, Major Bixby told the tale of how he'd almost won the Victoria Cross in the Boer War, while One-Eye Mulligan had his good eye bandaged and, blindfolded, challenged anybody to beat him at darts.

The tourists were enchanted and snapped pictures which they showed to captive audiences back home. If the tourists questioned the locals about how good the beer really was, or whether the major's story was entirely factual, the answers are not recorded. But nobody doubted One-Eye Mulligan's skill, and anyone could have told you that he'd been offered a music hall job as The Blind Darter and had turned it down because he hated to leave his village. He never failed to throw a "bull and two double tops" (that is to say, one bull's eye and two darts in the outer ring). He swore he could shoot an apple off a woman's head, if one of them would only give him an apple. None did.

Constable Dimwiddie, as one of the pleasanter aspects of his job, made a practice of stopping in at The Perfect Ace whenever he happened to be thirsty. By sheer luck he arrived at the pub only a couple of minutes after the tragedy depicted in the sketch opposite. He looked round the premises for a few seconds before he spotted the clue that told him the entire story.

What was the clue, and what was the story?

1. *Did the pub have a regular patronage?* Yes ☐ No ☐

2. *Did Major Bixby have a regular seat in the tavern?* Yes ☐ No ☐

3. *Did he have a good audience as he told his tale for the last time?* Yes ☐ No ☐

4. *Were the locals interested in his stories?* Yes ☐ No ☐

5. *Was One-Eye Mulligan a good marksman?* Yes ☐ No ☐

6. *How far apart are the two pictures?* A day or two ☐ One week ☐ Several weeks ☐

7. *Are there any significant differences between the two pictures?* Yes ☐ No ☐

8. *Was the major's death an accident?* Yes ☐ No ☐

9. *If your answer to (8) is "no", who do you think killed the major, and what was the evidence?*

ANSWERS PAGE 60

# OH MY GOD!

Constable Dimwiddie had a reputation for gallantry as well as good sense. The latter was not hard to understand in view of his ability to keep the criminal population of Abbington Frith within bounds, but the former relied on a certain incident involving the dowager dame, Mrs. Peacock.

She had invited him over for a tête à tête concerning the escapades of her nephew and heir, the child of her unfortunate sister Mavis. Mavis had run away from home with an unscrupulous and bogus French count who fathered her child. She was deserted and left destitute to bring up her son who grew up an anarchist, a thorn in the side of the French government and Mrs. Peacock. For, although his aunt had willed him all her money on her decease, he never stopped pestering her for an advance on his inheritance.

Mrs. Peacock was, like Constable Dimwiddie, an inveterate and intrepid butterfly collector. She had therefore proposed a short butterfly-hunting expedition in the local woods before returning to a heart to heart talk over tea and cakes.

Upon returning from their foray, they approached Mrs. Peacock's house, opened the door, and saw what you see in the picture. Mrs. Peacock cried out, "Oh My God!" and started to enter the room. Constable Dimwiddie grabbed her arm and yelled "Don't!". Then, remembering that she was a lady, he added "Madam!"

A few weeks later she sent him a diamond butterfly which was a masterpiece of the jeweller's art, and with it a note thanking him for saving her life.

What did he see, and how did he save her life?

**1.** *Do you think that this was the work of more than one person?* Yes ☐ No ☐

**2.** *Do you think that robbery was their real motive?* Yes ☐ No ☐

**3.** *Do you think they messed up the room on purpose?* Yes ☐ No ☐

**4.** *Could they have vandalized in order to mask another, more sinister, purpose?* Yes ☐ No ☐

**5.** *Did they move the rug?* Yes ☐ No ☐

**6.** *Did they hide something under the rug?* Yes ☐ No ☐

**7.** *Did Constable Dimwiddie suspect that it was something dangerous, like a bomb?* Yes ☐ No ☐

**8.** *Did he think that the vandals planned to kill Mrs. Peacock?* Yes ☐ No ☐

**9.** *Was the bomb the only danger in the room?* Yes ☐ No ☐. *If no, what other things in the area were dangerous?*

**10.** *Was Constable Dimwiddie able to provide a clue to the identity of at least one of the vandals?* Yes ☐ No ☐

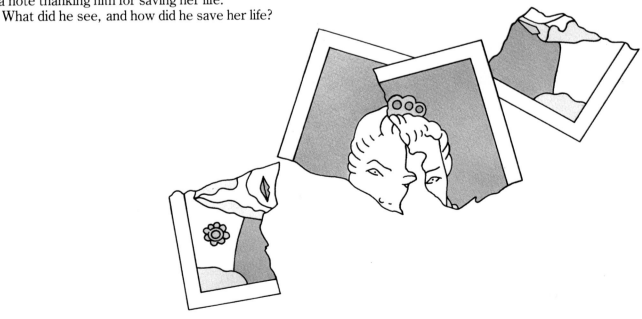

ANSWERS PAGE 60

# THE POWDER ROOM

It was the custom for the Thwackenham Hunt to hold its annual hunt ball at Tudor Close. This occasion was the highlight of the English social season, and therefore mandatory for anybody who was anybody to be seen there – no matter whether he or she knew one end of a horse from another. In addition to the cream of British society, the dance was also attended by diplomats posted to the various embassies in London. Mr Black, who had inherited the great house from his brother, was happy to continue the tradition.

One guest, a perennial, was the mysterious Felicia de Mendacia-Soar. Universally regarded as a beauty, she had swept her way through the ranks of diplomats picking up lovers and information – discarding the former when the latter dried up. In one way or another she had blackmailed most of them and become an international threat: women hated her and men feared her.

Therefore, when she was found dead in the powder room on the evening of the ball several people cheered, at least secretly. It was generally agreed that if anyone deserved to be poisoned, it was she. Constable Dimwiddie, however, had nothing to cheer about. Because of international considerations, he had to clear the matter up quickly, with as little interrogation as possible, and be sure he was right.

In this he had some assistance. Mrs. White, who had been brought back from retirement to serve as the attendant in the powder room, was able to pick out the four women who had used it between the time of Felicia's entrance and the discovery of her body. They were, in the order of their appearance, Miss Cynthia Scarlet, Señora Cordoba, Dame Winifred von Sims and Mademoiselle Fifi La France.

Knowing that time was precious, Constable Dimwiddie hoped that, if it was murder, the shock of being near the body would cause the guilty woman to give herself away. Therefore, he had the four suspects assemble in the powder room while he endeavoured to solve the case. Luck was with him and he didn't have too long to wait for the solution.

How long does it take you?

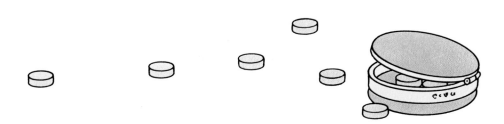

**1.** *Did Felicia commit suicide? Yes ☐ No ☐*

**2.** *Could she have been tricked into taking poison? Yes ☐ No ☐*

**3.** *Could the poison have been administered by someone other than the four women who were questioned? Yes ☐ No ☐*

**4.** *Would you regard Mrs. White as a suspect? Yes ☐ No ☐*

**5.** *Is the possession of a handbag a suspicious factor? Yes ☐ No ☐*

**6.** *Could the body have been carried or dragged to the linen chest after Felicia had collapsed from the fatal dose? Yes ☐ No ☐*

**7.** *Do you think the killer was physically strong? Yes ☐ No ☐*

**8.** *Is the last person to have gone into the powder room necessarily the killer? Yes ☐ No ☐*

**9.** *Who do you think killed Felicia?*

ANSWERS PAGE **60**

# INTO THIN AIR

The Countess Karamazova and her jewels were a source of gossip in Abbington Frith, and how she had managed to get her hands on what had once been a portion of the Russian crown jewels was a mystery. Professor Plum, Colonel Mustard and Reverend Green spent countless hours in The Perfect Ace talking about what they could do if only they could get their hands on the gems.

The countess was persuaded by members of the Robin Hood club to put her jewellery on show for charity – including the fabulous pendant weighing nearly thirty carats. Being generous and trusting, up to a point anyhow, and having over-insured them, she exhibited the jewels among the treasures at Tudor Close and let the good people of Abbington Frith stare, touch, and envy.

Special security guards were hired to stand watch over the jewel, but when some of a small boy's balloons exploded with a series of bangs and he went into a tantrum, they, as well as everyone in the room, turned around to find out what the trouble was. Then, seeing the countess, who was just making her entrance, the guards let their gazes linger. By the time they turned back, the pendant had disappeared.

The countess cried out, "My diamond! A king gave it to me." And under her breath she murmured, "It's irreplaceable; after all, how many kings are left – at least the kind who hand out diamonds."

The sketch shows the hall immediately after the pendant disappeared. Can you tell who swiped the pendant and how it disappeared?

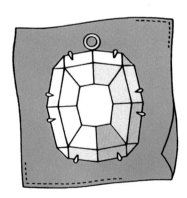

1. *Was it easy for Reverend Green to grab the pendant?* Yes ☐ No ☐

2. *Was it easy for Colonel Mustard to grab the pendant?* Yes ☐ No ☐

3. *Was it easy for Professor Plum to grab the pendant?* Yes ☐ No ☐

4. *Was it easy for one of the guards to grab the pendant?* Yes ☐ No ☐

5. *Do you see any likely place to hide the pendant during the few seconds after the balloons had burst?* Yes ☐ No ☐

6. *Was there any way of getting the pendant out of the room?* Yes ☐ No ☐

7. *Do you think that the balloons were burst accidentally?* Yes ☐ No ☐

8. *If no, was there something handy to cause this to happen?* Yes ☐ No ☐

9. *Do you think that the thief knew the balloons would burst?* Yes ☐ No ☐

10. *Do you think that the countess was party to the theft?* Yes ☐ No ☐

11. *Do you think that one of the security guards stole the pendant?* Yes ☐ No ☐

12. *If not, who do you think stole it and how can you tell?*

ANSWERS PAGE 61

# INTO THINNER AIR

When Constable Dimwiddie heard of the theft of the Countess Karamazova's pendant and was informed that Professor Plum had been in the room at the time, Dimwiddie's first thought was of Plum's madcap affair with Daphne Woodcock. It therefore seemed probable that Daphne had or would have the pendant. Moreover, he did have something quite definite to go on and that was the photograph that Reverend Green had taken. Out of focus it was, but it did seem to point to Professor Plum. Dimwiddie thought that he could just about make out the special signet ring he always wore.

Dimwiddie's job was to find the pendant. Since Daphne now lived in a nearby town where Dimwiddie had no jurisdiction, he phoned the local police and asked them to search Daphne and her home. Although the search produced nothing except several packets of letters involving a member of Parliament, an American millionaire and two sheikhs who were cousins, Dimwiddie was not satisfied.

He was, however, a romantic at heart, and he loved nothing better than a bit of adventure. Consequently, disguised as a chimney sweep and wearing a borrowed top hat, he climbed through a window in Daphne's house. Inside, he searched none of the usual places, since the local police had already covered them. Instead he stood for a few precious minutes surveying the room and letting his instincts take over. A few minutes later he left, with the pendant in his pocket.

Having heard various interesting things about the Countess Karamazova, he went straight to her house and presented her with the pendant. The Countess was properly grateful, but not quite so proper that Dimwiddie did not feel well rewarded.

Miss Daphne
Drounces
White Chi
Westl

The picture shows the portion of the room facing Dimwiddie when he decided where the pendant was. In which object was the pendant hidden, and how can you substantiate your choice?

*The book*

*The Staffordshire cat to the left*

*The Staffordshire cat to the right*

*The candlestick to the left*

*The candlestick to the right*

*The clock*

*The plant on the right*

*The plant on the left*

*The bun*

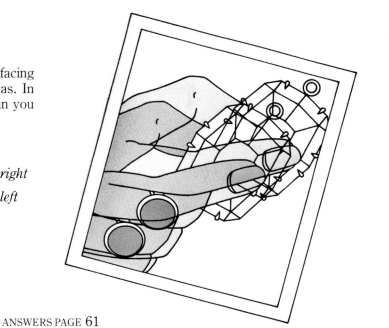

ANSWERS PAGE 61

# THE HARVEST SUPPER

Guy Brie, the Abbington Frith Gazette's chief reporter, had managed to injure or insult almost all the villagers. Colonel Mustard, for instance, had never forgiven Brie for reprinting his old acting reviews in a feature on the illustrious pasts of village residents. Professor Plum had little use for Brie after he had returned Rupert's photograph, entered in the Gazette's most beautiful baby competition, with "Are you kidding?" scrawled across it. Neither did Green have any feelings of friendship towards Brie, who was always hinting that the only vows that the Reverend Green took were marriage ones, and they were broken regularly every Tuesday and Saturday.

As for the ladies, Miss Scarlet seethed every time Brie snickered as she recounted her death-defying performance as the "Artiste of the Air". Mrs. Peacock was still smarting about his first article for the paper headlined – "Peacock, silly goose, ends up dead duck". While Mrs. White, cook extraordinaire, detested Brie's slanderous references to her cooking as "English slop".

Brie was aware of his unpopularity, but nevertheless he came to the village's annual harvest supper in high spirits. He did, however, remember to remind himself to be on his guard.

Wandering about the grounds, he nosed about for some news, then queued up at the buffet table. He helped himself to a full plate of Mrs. White's vegetable soup and sat down in the last available seat at the table. Laughing and joking while he ate and drank, he stopped suddenly, clutched at his throat, and collapsed, and died. The others, fearing a case of poisoning and unsure of what had been poisoned, jumped up and ran off.

Constable Dimwiddie who had been out after a particularly fine specimen of *Papilio machaon* (swallowtail butterfly), happened to stumble into the supper area. Although he was tired and hungry, he examined the evidence before daring to eat. Once he was sure of exactly what had happened, he sat down and gorged himself on Mrs. White's best. Then, on a full stomach, he was ready to make his charge. Whom did he accuse, and how did he arrive at his conclusion?

**1.** *Who were Brie's table companions, and where did they sit?*

**2.** *Did all of them have a motive for killing Guy?* Yes ☐ No ☐

**3.** *Was the killing carefully planned?* Yes ☐ No ☐

**4.** *Did the guests serve themselves, making their own choices?* Yes ☐ No ☐

**5.** *If Guy had been served by his neighbours, would he have been suspicious?* Yes ☐ No ☐

**6.** *Do you think the wine or cider was poisoned?* Yes ☐ No ☐

**7.** *Do you think the bread was poisoned?* Yes ☐ No ☐

**8.** *Do you think poison was put into Guy's food after he had served himself?* Yes ☐ No ☐

**9.** *Could one of the guests have added poison to his or her own food while pretending, for instance, to add salt or pepper?* Yes ☐ No ☐

**10.** *If someone had simply exchanged plates with Guy would he have been suspicious?* Yes ☐ No ☐

**11.** *Did somebody trick Guy into taking poisoned food?* Yes ☐ No ☐

**12.** *Is there any evidence of a trick, diversion or incident?* Yes ☐ No ☐

**13.** *How was Guy poisoned?*

ANSWERS PAGE 61

# FEMME FATALE

Henrietta Street, Cynthia Scarlet's American cousin, was sharp, shrewd and shapely. She had arrived one summer announcing that she needed a rest cure and that Abbington Frith was the place to have it. Not adverse, however, to doing a bit of business even in that "one-horse town", as she so quaintly put it, she continued to sell worthless stock and non-existent oil wells just as she had in Chicago, under the name of Diana, Limited.

One day she made three attempts at a sale, but she seriously misjudged her customers. Instead of making a deal, she ended up as you see her. Though her charlady occasionally had come upon Henrietta sleeping off the effects of the previous night, this time there were two notable differences – she was in the bath, and she was dead. As for the alcohol and sleeping pills, she'd been addicted to both.

Some notes scattered on the table gave the names of the men she'd expected to see on the previous day. All three readily admitted having seen Miss Street on the afternoon of her death and said the following:

Colonel Mustard was all bluster. "I?" he spluttered. "Involve myself with someone like her? Everything about her was vulgar. Offering me a cocktail the moment I came in, for instance – it's not done. Although I'd made an appointment with her to discuss some possible investments, I realized at once that she had something shady in mind. In order not to offend her when she poured the drinks, I accepted one, but when she started to talk about a newly discovered gold mine, I realized that her proposition was sheer swindle. At that, I excused myself as delicately as I could and went home."

Horatio Green said, "I think she planned to compromise me, or perhaps to get me drunk. Those Americans are not very subtle, you know. In any case I walked in to find the drinks laid out, with an obvious intention. When she got up to pour me a cocktail, which incidentally was quite warm and watery, I realized that she'd had too many already. She started to offer me some stock in an oil well that produced a quality so pure that it scarcely needed refining. That was enough to warn me to stay away from her, so I left."

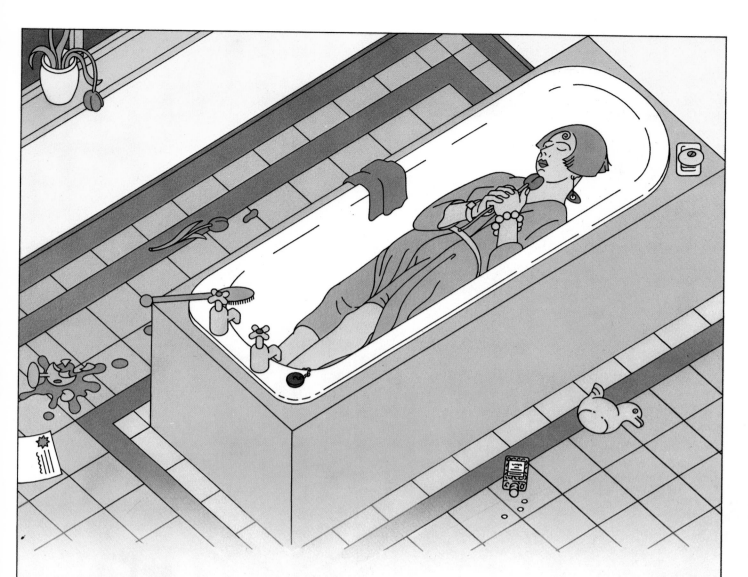

Professor Plum said, "When I arrived, she said that she was delighted that I'd come, she'd always wanted to meet me. That was a bit too effusive. I admit that I drank one cocktail with her, just one, but I was late for another appointment and I didn't even give her time to make her sales pitch. I confess that I left a bit abruptly."

Constable Dimwiddie sighed. He hated to think of Henrietta having done away with herself but it seemed the obvious explanation. Wouldn't you agree?

**1.** *Did Henrietta have a reason to feel depressed?*
*Yes* ☐ *No* ☐

**2.** *Had she had a lot to drink?* *Yes* ☐ *No* ☐

**3.** *Do you think there had been a scuffle?* *Yes* ☐ *No* ☐

**4.** *Had Henrietta committed suicide?* *Yes* ☐ *No* ☐

**5.** *Do you think she received her fatal injury in the bathtub?* *Yes* ☐ *No* ☐

**6.** *Do you think her death might have been accidental?*
*Yes* ☐ *No* ☐

**7.** *Could someone have carried her into the bathroom?*
*Yes* ☐ *No* ☐

**8.** *Would the purpose be to make it look like suicide?*
*Yes* ☐ *No* ☐

**9.** *Would the last man who saw her be the most likely suspect?* *Yes* ☐ *No* ☐

**10.** *Who was he?*

ANSWERS PAGE 61

# MEMORIES OF THE BULL RING

Mrs. Eudocia Plum had never forgiven her unfaithful husband his affair with the attractive Daphne Woodcock. When the scandal and rumours surrounding the theft of the Countess Karamazova's pendant died down, she dragged off the professor to a cold comfort farm on the outskirts of the village, and thereby ensured that he spent his days with only herself and the children as companions.

As for the three little Plums, they were a rambunctious lot, and delighted in playing games around the farm. Their favourite activity involved Old Ollie, rumoured to have been brought up for the bullring. His previous owner claimed he had gored several toreadors when young, but since arriving at the Plums, he showed no sign of emotion save for some heavy snorting when Eudocia appeared.

Constable Dimwiddie had to pass the Plums on his way to The Perfect Ace. It was his custom to leave his bicycle at their gatepost when he went to the pub, as this gave him some distance in which to walk off the effects of his drinking on the return trip. This particular hot summer's day was no different. As he placed his bicycle at the gatepost he saw the usual domestic scene – the little Plums playing, Eudocia complaining, and Plum looking resigned. But when he arrived back at the Plums' and to the scene on the right, Dimwiddie wondered whether he had had one pint too many. He sobered up quickly, however, as Plum explained that he'd returned from the fields to find his wife fatally wounded. He said he'd been in a state of shock ever since. What do you think were Dimwiddie's conclusions?

1. *Were the little Plums mischievous?*
Yes ☐ No ☐

2. *Was Professor Plum happily married?*
Yes ☐ No ☐

3. *Did Ollie have a blood-thirsty past?*
Yes ☐ No ☐

4. *Who had a motive for killing Eudocia?*
*Professor Plum ☐ The little Plums ☐*
*Ollie ☐*

5. *What possible weapons were there for*
*killing Eudocia?  Pitchfork ☐ Sword ☐*
*Horns ☐ Handlebars ☐*

6. *Is there blood on any of the above?*
Yes ☐ No ☐

7. *Did Ollie appear to be in a passive mood?*
Yes ☐ No ☐

8. *Did Ollie have reason to recall the heat*
*and glory of his youth, and might he have*
*acted accordingly?*  Yes ☐ No ☐

9. *Had Ollie moved?*  Yes ☐ No ☐

10. *Who killed Eudocia?*

ANSWERS PAGE 61

# A THREE PINT MYSTERY

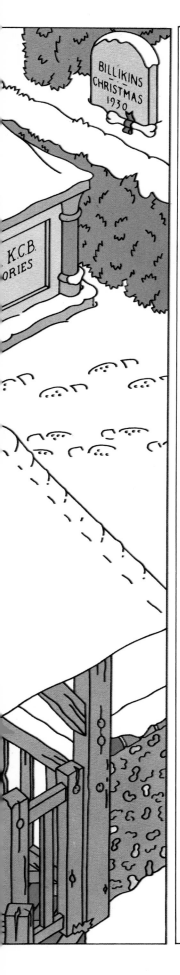

# TILL DEATH DO US PART

Lady Millicent Mountjoy was a scourge to her husband in death as in life. Instead of leaving him her fortune in a form that would have brought him not only release from her, but a wealthy old age, she left him penniless by willing that all her assets be converted to gold. This gold was to be used for a bust, with the face shaped by her death mask. Upon his death, her bust was to be placed in his coffin, doubtless so that she could supervise his existence throughout eternity. Trusting no one, she took precautions to ensure the bust against any possible theft before it reached its final resting place.

In due time, as she had so wisely foreseen, her husband Quentin Mountjoy died. The following day the Reverend Green, in his capacity of undertaker, put the body on view. Among those who came to pay their respects were Fabius Corpus (the family lawyer, recently crippled), Midshipman Sindbad (Quentin's nephew), Mrs. White, Mrs. Peacock, Miss Scarlet, Colonel Mustard, Professor Plum, and even Constable Dimwiddle, who perhaps smelt trouble.

However, nothing out of the ordinary happened, except that just before closing the coffin and in a spirit of childish playfulness, Green placed Quentin's inert arms around Lady Millicent's bust. Neither Fabius Corpus nor Colonel Mustard nor Professor Plum, who were watching, saw the humour of it. Somewhat embarrassed, Green closed the coffin and screwed it down. Shortly afterwards he followed the hearse to the cemetery, where he conducted a brief ceremony. Only Sindbad and Fabius Corpus attended.

The following night, Constable Dimwiddie was making his rounds when he noticed some lights in the churchyard. Yelling out "Who goes there?" he blundered around the corner of Sir Montague's tomb and stopped short. There, in the dawn's early light, he saw that Mountjoy's grave had been opened. On further investigation he found that Lady Millicent's golden bust was gone, all fifty pounds of it.

Constable Dimwiddie decided to question the three men present at the funeral on the previous day. After he had reviewed their statements, he felt he didn't need to look further. Can you, by studying the picture, decide whether their statements were true or false, and whether there was sufficient evidence to figure out who had gone off with Lady Millicent's bust?

**Sindbad said**   1. *"I only went to pay my respects at the grave site.* True ☐ False ☐ Insufficient evidence ☐

2. *"When I got there I saw Fabius jimmying open the coffin.* True ☐ False ☐ Insufficient evidence ☐

3. *"I then chased Fabius."* True ☐ False ☐ Insufficient evidence ☐

**Fabius said**   4. *"I only went to pay my respects at the grave site.* True ☐ False ☐ Insufficient evidence ☐

5. *"When I got there I saw Sindbad jimmying open the coffin.* True ☐ False ☐ Insufficient evidence ☐

6. *"I tried to stop him.* True ☐ False ☐ Insufficient evidence ☐

7. *"Sindbad ran off and I chased him.* True ☐ False ☐ Insufficient evidence ☐

8. *"I went back the way I came."* True ☐ False ☐ Insufficient evidence ☐

**Reverend Green said**   9. *"I did not visit the grave site that night.* True ☐ False ☐ Insufficient evidence ☐

10. *"There's plenty of evidence to show that Fabius and Sindbad stole the bust together.* True ☐ False ☐ Insufficient evidence ☐

11. *"The last time I saw the bust was when I closed the coffin lid."* True ☐ False ☐ Insufficient evidence ☐

12. *Who stole the bust?* Sindbad ☐ Fabius ☐ Green   ANSWERS PAGE 61

# MAKING TRACKS

Constable Dimwiddie had reached the end of his rope. Enough was enough! In his many years as protector of Abbington Frith's peace, he had steadfastly, even in the face of extremely strong evidence to the contrary, believed in the essential goodness of his fellow villagers. That is why he had never before made public his secret file, never before communicated his secret solutions. For years he had withstood the scorn of his superiors as they pondered one after the other of his cases which he had filed with "culprit unproven".

But somehow, in a way that he couldn't explain, it had all caught up with him. The perpetrators of the latest crime to befall Abbington Frith, Mr. Black's death, could no longer be ignored.

He had overlooked too many suspicious circumstances to allow the suspects to escape Scot-free. Even if he couldn't accuse the actual culprit of that particular incident, he had enough circumstantial evidence to put the lot away for life.

He, therefore, prepared himself thoroughly to face them. He gathered up all his notes, exhibits. eye-witness reports, photographs, drawings, scene-of-the-crime evidence, etc. and set them up in the study at Tudor Close. Then the evening before he had planned to confront them all, he sent around individual notes kindly, but firmly, requesting that Miss Cynthia Scarlet, Mrs. Penelope Peacock, Colonel Ivor Mustard, Professor Albert Plum, Reverend Horatio Green and Mrs. Beryl White assemble at Tudor Close where he would reveal all. However, when he arrived at the appointed hour, the house was empty and the study had been completely ransacked. All his notes exhibits, eye-witness reports, photographs, drawings, scene-of-the-crime evidence, etc. were all gone. Without wasting a moment he ran out of the house and down the drive and was met by the following scene.

Although he spent many fruitless hours scouring Abbington Frith and wiring for information from nearby towns and villages, no trace of the miscreants were to be found. His only lead, therefore, was the rather confusing scene he had first met at the drive. There certainly were a wealth of clues, but what did they all mean? Was he going to be able to explain not only how they had all gotten away, but where they were all headed? Could you?

*Miss Scarlet*
*She probably will be found at*

*Professor Plum*
*Look for him in*

*Colonel Mustard*
*He's most likely in*

*Mrs. White*
*You'll find her*

*Reverend Green*
*He's sure to be discovered in*

*Mrs. Peacock*
*I warrant she'll be*

ANSWERS PAGE 64

# IN THE ACT II

The answers to the questions on page 29 are irrelevant and may be answered any way you wish. The purpose of the puzzle is to test the accuracy of your observation. If you were a witness to an actual crime or accident, how well would you be able to describe the people involved?

As a test of your ability to describe the thief, answer the questions below, but **do not look back** at the picture of the theft. After you've finished, you can check your answers by turning back to the sketch and deciding for yourself which of your answers were right.

*Age:*
*Under 40 ☐ 40-60 ☐ Over 60 ☐*
*Height:*
*Under 6 feet ☐ Over 6 feet ☐*
*Weight:*
*Thin ☐ Medium ☐*
*Overweight ☐*
*Identifying marks:*
*Birthmark ☐*
*Scars ☐*
*Wearing a ring?*
*Yes ☐ No ☐*
*Colour of eyes:*
*Blue ☐ Brown ☐*
*Black ☐*
*Lips:*
*Full ☐ Thin ☐*
*Lower lip bulging ☐*
*Ears:*
*Small ☐ Close to head ☐*
*Large lobes ☐*
*Face shape:*
*Round ☐ Oval ☐ Square ☐*

*Was he wearing a hat? Yes ☐ No ☐*
*Beret ☐ Flat cap ☐*

*Was his hair*
*Curly ☐ Short ☐ Slicked down ☐ Dishevelled ☐*

 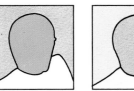   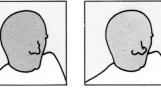 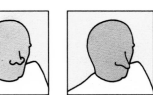
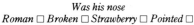

*Was he bald?*
*Slightly ☐ Completely ☐*

*Was his nose*
*Roman ☐ Broken ☐ Strawberry ☐ Pointed ☐*

  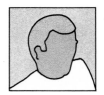 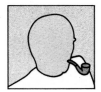 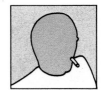 

*Was his colouring*
*Medium with blonde hair ☐ Flushed with brown hair ☐*
*Swarthy with grey hair ☐*

*Was he smoking? Yes ☐ No ☐*
*Pipe ☐ Cigarette ☐ Cigar ☐*

*Was he wearing glasses? Yes □ No □*
*Horn rims □ Dark glasses □ Half frames □*

*Was he clean shaven? Yes □ No □ Trimmed moustache □*
*Full moustache □ Moustache and beard □*

*What was he wearing around his neck?*
*Tie □ Scarf □ Bowtie □ Nothing □*

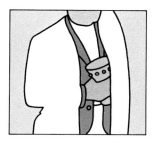   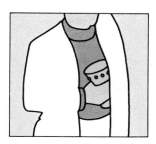

*What was he wearing under his coat?*
*Green jacket □ Blue suit □ Grey suit □ Blue jersey □*

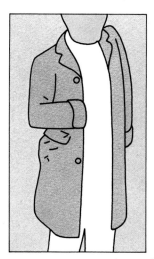   

*What kind of coat did he wear? Grey overcoat □ Raincoat □ Blue overcoat □*
*Dark coat with fur collar □ Was the collar turned up? Yes □ No □*

  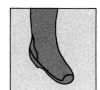   

*Were his trousers Brown □ Grey □ Did they have turn-ups? Yes □ No □*
*Was he wearing Boots □ Brown shoes □ Blue shoes □ Were they clean? Yes □ No □*

# ANSWERS

## THE VANDALS

*1. Yes because the cash box is almost empty.*

*2. No. Kids love picnics, and probably you do, too.*

*3. Yes, there is too much damage to believe that it was done by a single nine-year-old.*

*4. Yes. The desk in the lower left-hand corner (Professor Plum's) and the bottom shelf of the bookcase are apparently untouched.*

*5. No, because the marks are in the wrong place, near the keyhole and not near the top of the drawer and lock.*

*6. With a key. There are no scratches or other indications that the cash box has been tampered with.*

*7. No, because none of the objects shown could have been used to open the drawer or cash box. Peter's keys are not the type that would fit this desk.*

*8. Professor Plum, because he was poor and had to match the entire fund.*

*9. Constable Dimwiddie had little trouble with this case. In fact, it fits in with the first and second requirements of an investigation, to wit; whoever commits a crime must have both motive and opportunity. Therefore, was it Hugo Furst, Peter Peacock III or little Johnny White? Solution p.62*

## AT THE BOATHOUSE

*1. Yes, things like this have been known to have happened.*

*2. No. The rope was cleanly cut, rather than torn, and is wound through the chair. An overturned chair proves nothing.*

*3. No. This depends entirely on his own say-so.*

*4. No. Nobody would heat a room on a summer's day. The fire was probably lit to destroy evidence.*

*5. Yes. The broken mallet, and fragments of letters, are strongly suggestive of a quarrel.*

*6. No. The broken mallet looks suspicious, but the lab report proved that a metal object, not a wooden one, caused the wound.*

*7. No. It would be almost impossible to do this without damaging the guard rail or getting blood on the bottom surface.*

*8. Yes, easily.*

*9. No, because he would have been within sight of the croquet players all the time.*

*10. Yes. There are spots of fresh blood mixed in with the red paint stains. The differing tints of red so indicate.*

*11. Constable Dimwiddie certainly thought that Wilmot had killed Percy. The blood stains, cut rope and fire were extremely suspicious and did not fit in with Wilmot's explanation. Dimwiddie also knew very well that a clue may be something which is not present, and should be, as well as something which is there and should not be. By careful study of the scene, you should be able to discover the missing weapon and thus reconstruct the crime. Solution p.62*

## WITCHCRAFT

*1. Yes, it was Hallowe'en.*

*2. Yes. A collector of voodoo items is likely to be.*

*3. Yes. The three hats, plus the multiplicity of other objects, prove the recent presence of several people.*

*4. Yes, as evidenced by the hats and broomstick.*

*5. No. His collection consisted of rare and unusual voodoo pieces, whereas the things on the stairs were not of this type.*

*6. No. Any kid can tell you that the hats are too big and that most of the stuff is not the usual cheap, commercial merchandise normally worn or carried by "trick-or-treaters".*

*7. Yes. The shots came from fireworks, the evidence of which is on the stairs.*

*8. Yes. The various articles on the steps are calculated to cause fright. The entire Hallowe'en tradition would reinforce such an effect.*

*9. Yes. There was no evidence of any assault.*

*10. No. Whoever came had criminal intent. It was not too difficult to discover that Penn had a heart condition, was superstitious and lived alone in an isolated spot. A group of shrieking, menacing "witches" would scare anyone.*

*11. Yes, definitely. This was a well-thought-out operation and carried out by a group. It was also a professional job. The clues to the identities of the perpetrators are in plain view. Whom would you accuse? Solution p.62*

## THE DEATH OF BILLIKINS

*1. Yes, judging by their collars, treats, bows, grooming accessories and picture frames.*

*2. Yes, since they ate and played together.*

*3. Yes.*

*4. Yes, there were food scraps in the garbage.*

*5. Yes, some of the gardening supplies are poisonous.*

*6. No, there is no evidence to support such a theory; all the garden poisons are sealed and topped by undisturbed snow.*

*7. Yes. The mistletoe in the garbage can is extremely poisonous.*

*8. Even an indulgent Mrs. White had to admit the snap-shots were not the best, but they did provide all the evidence. Since there is no indication that Billikins was deliberately poisoned, although there are poisoning agents about, somehow a poison must have been available to Billikins. By juggling the photographs around to show the sequence of events, Mrs. White was able to pinpoint the exact instance. Have you been able to do the same? Solution p.62*

## NOT A PRETTY SIGHT

*1. True.*

*2. False. The game was faked because, although pen and pencil were available, only the pen was used, and apparently by the same hand.*

*3. False, there were three almost empty bottles.*

*4. False. The unused plates and napkins, and lack of crumbs show that they ate nothing.*

*5. Impossible to prove. We have only his say-so, though wine and sun might make anyone fall asleep.*

*6. True.*

*7. False. All the evidence points to their incompatibility – his fine appearance, her loudness; his neatness, her messiness; his tastefulness, her vulgarity; his trimness, her fatness; his youth, her age…*

*8. False. The above incompatibility is a good reason.*

*9. Impossible to prove, as it depends entirely on his word. The purse, however, is missing.*

*10. Impossible to prove, as above, but it would be like Vanessa to wear a fur coat to a picnic.*

*11. False. If that was the motive, why did the killer neglect to take her jewellery?*

*12. Constable Dimwiddie certainly didn't find Horatio's case convincing. He thought he knew what happened; do you? Solution p.62*

## LOVERS' LEAP

*1. Yes, that is its purpose.*

*2. No. The fact that she was dressed up and had brought her passport with her indicates she was expecting something quite different from death.*

*3. Yes, judging by her loose shoe, broken heel and the piece of shirting that she still holds in her hand.*

*4. No. All the notes lying about are "ones", while Dr. Brunhilder's were of larger denominations.*

*5. Yes, as any smart thief would.*

*6. No. There are no blood stains and the second bullet punctured the sign.*

*7. No. The way the fence is broken, with the damaged rail pushed towards the body, is not consistent with the suicide theory of someone crashing through the fence.*

*8. Yes. He could have gone back the way he came, or, judging by the sign on the tree, "tough climb", he could have gone down the hard way.*

*9. Yes. As your answers suggest, Homer hid most of the five thousand pounds which he intended to spend on himself and the green-eyed parlour maid. But he soon found out that two can't live as expensively as one, so he hit on a better idea, namely to fake a suicide pact. To carry it out, he wrote the note to the police, shot his girlfriend and hoped that the police would think he'd flung himself over the cliff. But, if you think Homer's living on easy street, you would be wrong. What do you think happened to spoil his plan? Solution p.62*

## ALL IN GOOD FUN

*There were 14 practical jokes including:*

*1. A flour sack placed on top of the door.*

*2. Billiard balls glued to the table.*

*3. A tomato instead of a billiard ball.*

*4. A trip wire attached to the billiard table.*

*5. A nail fixed on to the cue stick.*

*6. A pool table pocket cut open.*

*7. A chair leg sawed through.*

*8. The parrot set free from its cage.*

*9. The caged hare.*

*10. French fries garnishing the fish.*

*11. Paint smeared on the portrait.*

*12. The twisted suit of armour.*

*13. A tack on the seat of the chair.*

*14. Banana skin on the floor.*

Ecclestrip's death was not a practical joke – it was an accident. The members of the Robin Hood club always did things in good fun and wouldn't have had murder as a motive. Besides, the chances of Ecclestrip dying from slipping on the banana skin and striking his head were so remote as to be unintentional. Therefore, there were only 14 acts of sabotage, and the member's number was 14.

But when Dimwiddie enquired as to the identity of number 14 he was told it was against club rules to divulge it. However, because of the serious consequences of the deed, he received the following clue:

"If you are after the pick of the bunch or the unripe one, you're miles off, but one below the leaf and you may be hot on the trail."

Who was number 14 – Mustard, Green or Plum? Solution p.62.

## UNDER THE BIG TOP

*1. Yes, otherwise there would have been a number of footsteps and prints.*

*2. Yes. The pattern of the footsteps matches the soles of McNiff's boots.*

*3. No, because he had a lighted cigar.*

*4. No. His walking pattern is undisturbed and his gun is still in his waistband, and besides it was dark.*

*5. No, because the bullet travelled straight down, whereas, if fired from the aerialist's perch, it would have entered McNiff's head at an angle.*

*6. No. Assuming Cynthia was the only one capable of even attempting such a feat, it was well-known that she could see but a foot in front of her nose even at high noon.*

*7. No, because there were no hoofprints in the ring.*

*8. Constable Dimwiddie knew from his investigation that the fatal shot must have been fired from a height. Judging by the condition of most of the performers he felt there was really only one person both physically as well as professionally capable of performing such a feat. Was it Jake, Cynthia, Ethel, Sandy or Johannes? Solution p.62*

## TENNIS, ANYONE?

*1. No, Nigel had brown eyes and Neville blue.*

*2. No, the body was at their backs.*

*3. Yes, one of the statements is obviously true.*

*4. Yes, because they made identical statements, indicating that they had rehearsed their answers.*

*5. No. There is a suspicious-looking stain near Nigel's pocket, but as he so innocently explained, the stain was from his Bloody Mary.*

*6. No. If it had been premeditated, the killer would have brought a weapon with him. Instead, he became angry and picked up the nearest weapon, which happened to be a rock.*

*7. While taking their statements, Constable Dimwiddie noticed eight possible indications of right- and left-handedness. Although he didn't need it, he secured one further proof. This clinched the case for the constable. He knew that if a right-hander had thrown the stone, it would have wounded Caspar on the right side of the head, knocked him forward and to the left of the path. Therefore, the murderer had to be left-handed. Was this Neville or Nigel? Solution p.63*

## PEACOCK'S POSER

*1. New Year's Eve, because he picked up his paper on the morning of December 31st, but failed to on the morning of January 1st.*

*2. Yes.*

*3. No.*

*4. Yes.*

*5. No, there is no evidence of a search.*

*6. Yes. His gun was used and taken from the wall, and is now in his hand. Furthermore, the door is bolted from the inside.*

*7. Yes, notice his apron.*

*8. Yes.*

*9. Yes. He had set the calendar forward in the expectation of seeing the following day; he was in the middle of cooking; he was reading the financial section and had a note to phone his broker. These are the actions of a man who expected to live. Finally, why would he have rolled back the rug and turned out the light if he expected to commit suicide?*

*10. Yes.*

*11. Constable Dimwiddie knew all about locked room mysteries, and all he had to do to prove it was murder was to figure out how the murderer had bolted the door from the outside. Careful scrutiny of the door revealed all to him – does it to you? Solution p.63*

## TRIAL RUN

*1. No, there is no evidence of a hidden camera.*

*2. Yes.*

*3. No. The lock was operated from the inside, and the long bolt could be raised easily.*

*4. No. From what is seen at first glance, the garden wall is low enough to climb over easily.*

*5. He saw something which made him realize the room was a trap. Do you know what it was? Solution p.63*

## APHRODITE'S REVENGE

1. Yes. His gun and flashlight indicate that he thought a burglar was in the house. The broken pane indicates why he thought so.

2. Yes. The window was broken from the inside, apparently with a book, as all the glass lies outside on the patio.

3. Yes. Each was due for a substantial inheritance upon Sir Montague's death.

4. No. She was pushed. Both the pedestal and the bust itself were too solid and heavy to tip accidentally. If the bust had fallen accidentally, it would lie closer to its pedestal.

5. No, because he was hit on the back of the head.

6. No. The gun went off accidentally when he was knocked down, otherwise it would not have been so off target, as shown by the bullet hole just below the ceiling moulding.

7. No. It would serve no useful purpose there.

8. No, because the edge of the material is smooth, as if cut by scissors, rather than ragged, as if by a tear. Moreover, the position of the nail near the bottom of the door makes it highly unlikely that anyone's jacket could have brushed up against it.

9. Yes, because the statue and doorknob are stained with chocolate, as if held by hands that held the eclair which lies crushed in front of the door.

10. Yes, because the bit of cloth must have been nailed on purpose to the door, and the window broken deliberately in order to bring Sir Montague downstairs.

11. The person who committed this murder not only was strong but knew enough about the other suspects to plant evidence against them. This being the case was the murderer Stanley "Solly" Zambesi, Miss Scarlet or Selwyn? Solution p.63

## THE KIDNAPPED KID

1. Yes, because the windows were boarded up and various preparations had been made, such as placing the bolt at the top of the door, and stocking up on food supplies.

2. No. The door was fastened with a bolt which was too high for Rupert to have reached.

3. No. They boarded up the windows so that he couldn't describe the room or give its location.

4. No. The door has a very high bolt, he kept his knife in a place only he could reach, and his clothes were hung at an unusually great height. Judging by the bedding on the cot on the left, the occupant's feet stuck out at the end, as if he was too tall for the bed.

5. Yes, judging by his wide shoes, sagging bed and stretched suit.

6. No. His clothes – a three-piece suit, wide ties, and especially braces – are those of an older man.

7. Yes. The objects in the room are without clutter.

8. Yes. He left a suitcase and some clothes behind, and he left the radio on.

9. Red. Constable Dimwiddie had enough experience of small boys to notice a clue, even if it was misspelt. What would you do in a dark room with the pepper pot?

10. Yes, judging by the feeding bowl.

11. The kidnapper was blind. The boarded-up windows, the dog, the neat order with everything in place, as if set up to be recognized by touch, and most importantly, the lack of light bulbs, bear witness to a blind man.

12. More than one. A blind man cannot drive. For Constable Dimwiddie's complete description, see p.63.

## A MATTER OF GRAVITY

1. Yes.

2. Yes, apparently.

3. No. The jack handle is missing.

4. Probably not.

5. No, because apparently the Speedster never even moved.

6. Yes, judging by the cigarette ends.

7. Yes, because the grass has been trampled down and has not yet sprung back to its upright position. Also, there are greasy marks on the stile post.

8. Yes.

9. Yes, grudge motives. Val Haller had testified against Dr. Brunhilder in a malpractice suit and Mrs. White said it was common knowledge that she and the doctor didn't get along.

10. Constable Dimwiddie saw at once it wasn't an accident – too many things didn't ring true (see answers to questions 3, 5 and 6). But although he had two suspects with good motives, only one seemed to tie in with all the evidence – was this Mrs. White or Val Haller. Solution p.63

## THE PERFECT ACE

1. Yes. Judging by the two pictures, he sat on the same stool in the same place both times.

2. Yes, he's in the same place in both pictures.

3. No. The pub had only a handful of its regular customers.

4. No, they seem bored.

5. Yes. Careful study shows that his May fling of darts was duplicated in July.

6. Several weeks, judging by the calendar.

7. Yes. In the second sketch there are fewer customers in the pub, and the metal toe-stop has been moved to the left.

8. No. One-Eye Mulligan was too good a marksman to miss, and his darts in both pictures, even though months apart in time, hit at exactly the same height and relative position, though moved to the left in the second.

9. No. Motive and opportunity are the two most important elements in solving a crime. Dimwiddie reasoned that somebody not only gained substantially from the major's departure, but had the time and means to bring it about. Solution p.63.

## OH MY GOD!

1. Yes. Most of the room was disturbed in the short time Mrs. Peacock was out of her house.

2. No, because they left a number of valuable articles on the side table and bureau top, such as the small china and silver containers, the silver candlestick and chalice.

3. Yes.

4. Yes.

5. Yes. Note the difference in colour of the flooring, which was previously covered by the rug and is now exposed.

6. Yes, judging by the hump.

7. Yes, which is why he kept Mrs. Peacock from entering the room.

8. Yes.

9. No. In addition to Constable Dimwiddie's suspected bomb, there is also evidence that the tea milk had been poisoned (viz. the dead cat), that the tree limb bearing the swing was sawn through, a poisonous spider in the butterfly collection and a snake in the drapes, and that her portrait and rocking chair were booby-trapped.

10. Yes. Judging by the unusual presence of two items not normally found in the average English household, he advised his fellow officers to be on the lookout for . . . . . Solution p.63

## THE POWDER ROOM

1. No. You can't commit suicide and then dump yourself into a linen chest, and surely a woman as exotic as Felicia would not choose a humble linen chest for a final resting place.

2. Yes. Someone might have put poison into her glass. These women were smart, and could easily trick you or me. Me, anyhow.

3. Yes. Mrs. White was not necessarily telling the truth when she said that only four women had entered the powder room during the crucial period.

4. Yes. Anyone on the scene would have to be viewed with suspicion.

5. No, because the poison might have consisted of a minute quantity which could have been concealed anywhere. Besides, almost every woman carries a handbag.

6. Yes, and probably was.

7. Yes; physical strength was necessary to lift and carry Felicia to the chest.

8. No, because the body could easily have been overlooked in the linen chest while the ladies came and went.

9. Constable Dimwiddie had no trouble. He figured that only a very strong person could have lifted Felicia up and dumped her into the linen chest. This being the case, was the guilty party Mrs. White, Cynthia Scarlet, Señora Cordoba, Dame Winifred von Sims or Mademoiselle Fifi La France? Solution p.63

## INTO THIN AIR

1. Yes.

2. Yes.

3. Yes.

4. Yes.

5. Yes, in the chandelier.

6. Yes, through the open window.

7. No. It seems quite unlikely that two balloons would burst simultaneously.

8. Yes, the pointed spear of the other exhibit.

9. Yes, in fact he counted on it. He needed an accomplice to create a diversion.

10. No. She was too fond of her diamonds to plot their loss, and the remark you happened to hear made under her breath more or less indicates her shock and surprise. Besides, she knew she might have been caught, so why take chances? She was sure of having either the diamonds or the insurance money, and thus either way she was a winner.

11. No. He'd certainly be aware that he'd be the first one suspected.

12. This theft required planning and its method of execution was ingenious. While three other people could have grabbed the pendant, only one did and he has an obvious link with another participant in the picture. Study the scene carefully, then point your finger at the guilty party. Solution p.64

## INTO THINNER AIR

1. Not the book, since it's too small to accommodate the pendant.

2. Neither of the Staffordshire cats. The one on the left is cracked but was repaired long ago.

3. Neither of the candlesticks. Both are too narrow.

4. Not the clock. It is made primarily of glass and the jewel would be visible.

5. Possibly either of the plants, since they are both large enough to take the pendant, but this is the first place the police would search.

6. This would leave... Solution p.64

## THE HARVEST SUPPER

1. The obvious clues left on or near the table place Mrs. Peacock to Brie's left with Mrs. White just beyond, and Colonel Mustard to his right. Opposite him, from left to right, were Reverend Green, Miss Scarlet and Professor Plum.

2. Yes.

3. Yes, because the poison had to be brought in ahead of time without arousing suspicion.

4. Yes. The food was laid out on a buffet table.

5. Yes. Since nobody liked him, it would certainly arouse his curiosity, if not his suspicion.

6. No. Everyone at the table had apparently drunk either wine or cider with no known harmful effects.

7. No, for the same reason as above – none of the others was poisoned.

8. Yes. In no other way could he alone have been poisoned.

9. Yes, the action would seem perfectly normal.

10. Yes, wouldn't you be?

11. No, there is no other credible explanation.

12. Yes. The stains on the tablecloth are suspicious and indicate a minor mishap.

13. This was an audacious killing. To murder somebody in full sight of many witnesses testifies to the great cunning of the culprit. Therefore, to Constable Dimwiddie, it was all the more surprising that the killer had left behind an obvious clue to his method. By what simple device had Brie been persuaded to hand over his plate? Solution p.64

## FEMME FATALE

1. Yes. She had failed three times to make a sale.

2. Yes.

3. Yes. The stock certificates were scattered and torn, one of the bottles was knocked over, and her Diana was broken.

4. No. She has a wound on the back of her head – you can see the blood beneath her earring.

5. No. Judging by the blood stains she was killed in the living room.

6. Yes. There's blood on the corner of the table, which someone might easily fall against with disastrous consequences.

7. Yes, and evidently did.

8. Yes, especially if someone also placed the pills and drinks where they were found.

9. Obviously yes.

10. Constable Dimwiddie was familiar with Treat's law which states that the more you drink, the drunker you get. Henrietta was well into her cups by the time her third and last visitor arrived. Was this Plum, Mustard or Green? Solution p.64

## MEMORIES OF THE BULL RING

1. Yes. They probably turned the sign upside down, teased the bull and sabotaged the bicycle.

2. No.

3. Yes, he was said to have gored several toreadors.

4. All of them. Plum who had surely borne her nagging long enough; the children whom she was bawling out; and Ollie, with or without reason.

5. Sword, pitchfork or horns could make puncture wounds. The handlebars could not penetrate.

6. No.

7. Yes.

8. Yes. The children's teasing might easily have goaded him into the character of the fighting bull for which he was said to have been bred.

9. No. There are no new hoof prints near the body.

10. Ollie hasn't moved, and his horns are too far apart to have gored Eudocia. Nevertheless there is clear evidence as to what must have happened.

## TILL DEATH DO US PART

1. False. He had brought his duffle bag with him, probably to transport the bust. His footsteps encircle the open grave and descend into it.

2. *False. Fabius' footsteps never reached the coffin.*

3. *False. Sindbad's footsteps do not follow Fabius'.*

4. *False, judging by the spade that he brought with him.*

5. *True. Sindbad's footsteps approach the grave and descend into it.*

6. *True. There are marks indicating a scuffle, and Fabius' cane is broken.*

7. *False, Fabius' footprints do not follow Sindbad's.*

8. *False. There are no footsteps to show how he left. Therefore he must have been carried, obviously by Sindbad whose footsteps are deeper from the weight of his burden. He probably carried Fabius piggyback, which also accounts for his hat lying near the lychgate, as if knocked off by the roof.*

9. *True. There are no footprints to indicate his presence.*

10. *False. There is no evidence to show that they either stole the bust or acted together. They arrived from different directions and each brought a crowbar and spade. Furthermore, they obviously had a fight.*

11. *Insufficient evidence; we have only his say-so.*

12. *The ransacked coffin, the mess of footprints, and the sticks and shovels told only too clear a tale. The fact that everybody lied was less important to Constable Dimwiddie than interpreting the evidence correctly. Who was the guilty man? – Sindbad, Fabius Corpus or Reverend Green? Solution p. 64*

# SOLUTIONS

## THE VANDALS

**Professor Plum** stole the money. Not only did he have the best motive, but he was the only one capable of causing the damage to the top book shelves and upper wall, which are too high for any nine-year-old to reach. A nine-year-old would have disturbed the books on the lower shelves, which are seemingly untouched. More importantly, Plum had the keys to both the cash box and drawer.

If you were fooled by all the apparent schoolboy damage, Constable Dimwiddie wasn't. He guessed that the sabotage was an attempt to mislead him, especially because the screwdriver marks on the drawer were in the wrong place. Had it been forced open, the bolt of the lock would be up and the edge of the drawer would be badly chipped. Since it wasn't, Dimwiddie accused Plum, who learnt that small-time thievery was hardly worth while. Thus educated, he made an important decision: either marry wealth or else steal a fortune. But preferably both.

## AT THE BOATHOUSE

The poker from the fireplace set is missing and is an obvious weapon.

It would seem that in the course of a quarrel, Wilmot hit Percy on the back of the head with the poker then flung it in to the lake; drops of blood from the poker fell next to the red paint. After disposing of the weapon, Wilmot took blood from Percy's wound and smeared it on the base of the fireplace set, but he made the mistake of placing it where it could not have made contact with Percy's skull without damaging the rather flimsy rail on the base of the set. He then tipped over the chair, cut the rope, positioned the body, and finally built a fire in which he tossed those letters of Mercedes which he thought might be incriminating. After coolly surveying the scene, he rushed out of the boathouse and pretended to be in shock.

Constable Dimwiddie had the lake dragged. The poker was found about forty feet out, which is still a club record for poker-tossing.

## WITCHCRAFT

Members of the cast of Macbeth. Before Penn's recent disappearance from the drama pages, he managed a scathing review of the play. The result put all concerned out of work. Writing of Ivor Mustard (nicknamed "The Colonel" after he starred in *Gone With The Wine*), Penn concluded that he was "the worst Shakespearean actor of his generation, declaiming in a voice that almost reached the second row orchestra."

While no great shakes as an actor, Col. Mustard fancied he knew something about fright, especially stage fright. With full knowledge of Penn's known superstition and recent illness, he pursuaded his fellow actors to put on the performance of their lives on that fateful night. Somehow, away from the theatre, all that menacing shrieking came through as a direct threat to Penn, and his enfeebled heart gave out. Literally, he was scared to death.

## THE DEATH OF BILLIKINS

Placed in their proper order, the photographs show the two dogs sharing a meal, passing the garden shed, playing in front of the garbage can (two photos), and, finally, the dead Billikins. Mrs. White was able to point out that the track of the paw prints, the chewed-up turkey leg and the ravaged mistletoe indicated that Billikins, unkissed under the mistletoe, had decided to eat it – with disastrous results.

## NOT A PRETTY SIGHT

Much of this case depended on Horatio's evidence, much of which can neither be proved or disproved.

When Constable Dimwiddie stumbled on the body he could see that even in death Vanessa had no taste, and must have been a living nightmare to Horatio. Dimwiddie assumed rightly that Horatio had plied Vanessa with wine and waited until she fell asleep in the sun, then he inscribed the book and wrote out the tic-tac-toe marks though he forgot to use the pencil which he had so carefully placed alongside the paper. He then strangled her, took most of the food and went punting. He found that his appetite was gone, so he dropped the food overboard and kept on poling until he saw the body had been found. Then he punted gracefully back.

## LOVERS' LEAP

Homer's plan went awry when he couldn't find the key to the safe deposit box in the railway station where he had hidden the money. The magpie had taken it while Homer was busy faking the evidence. With a possible murder charge hanging over him, he couldn't risk being caught at the railway station. He therefore escaped under a new name and went back to butlering in Nicaragua. The brown-eyed Spanish parlour maid he found crass, and in due time he sickened and died.

On his death bed he said, "Crime does not pay." The parlour maid, hoping to hear what he'd done, said, "Can't you say something more original?"

He couldn't.

## ALL IN GOOD FUN

**Colonel Mustard.**

## UNDER THE BIG TOP

From the answers to the questions, most of the performers would have had difficulty shooting anything from a height, and certainly McNiff's demise was neatly accomplished. The small, round holes next to McNiff's footsteps were Constable Dimwiddie's main clue. These marks were made by stilts, and the long trousers hanging up are obviously those of a stilt man. Clowns are usually experts on stilts, as any child will tell you, even if you don't ask, and wasn't Sandy called the "Candystripe" clown? When Constable Dimwiddie made his arrest, Sandy admitted he'd planned his action well in advance.

Thoroughly familiar with McNiff's nocturnal habits, Sandy had waited until the bed check was over. Then he made his way back to the tent, donned his stilts and waited quietly in the pitch darkness at the edge of the ring. When McNiff came tramping noisily into the tent, Sandy stalked him until he stood over McNiff and his lighted cigar. Sandy fired one shot. Then, content that he'd avenged Cynthia, he went to bed and slept peacefully until he awoke to find Dimwiddie standing over him.

"First time I ever fired a loaded gun," Sandy said. Dimwiddie's comment was terse. "And the last," he said.

## TENNIS, ANYONE?

Neville. Full marks if you found all the signs that point to Neville's being left-handed, and Nigel right-handed:

Nicotine stains on Nigel's right hand
Ink stains on Neville's left hand
Handkerchief in Nigel's right-hand pocket
Drink in Nigel's right hand
Neville pouring drink with left hand
Hair partings on different sides
Wristwatches on opposite hands
Pencil behind Nigel's right ear

The clincher? their signatures! While signing their statements, Constable Dimwiddie saw immediately that Neville was left-handed.

It is well-known that twins have a lot of things in common, and these two shared a natural desire to avoid prosecution. Their best defense was a united front. Unfortunately, a united front was not an identical one, and Constable Dimwiddie was able to distinguish readily one from the other. But he was able to reassure them that they'd be together for at least a while longer. Neville, who had bashed Caspar and then rushed back to work things out with Nigel, was going to have his brother for a cell-mate. As Constable Dimwiddie pointed out, an accessory to homicide bears the same guilt as the principal.

## PEACOCK'S POSER

One of the two nuts used to hold the fastening screws on the back of the door is missing and is on Peacock's desk. This screw hole is in a perfect position to manipulate a wire from the outside through to the bolt. (That missing piece of fence was bent into shape and pushed through the screw hole to pull the bolt home once the door was closed.)

Constable Dimwiddie also had a hunch about the rolled-back rug. Whoever moved it did so to keep any blood from staining it and lowering its value. This pointed to one of Winston's heirs, and, most likely to **Penelope Peacock**, his only surviving female relation. And, in fact, it was she who had come round before dinner-time to help Winston see the year out.

## TRIAL RUN

He saw a moon with points facing to the left (first quarter), whereas the moon in its last quarter, which was the time he was planning to commit the crime, faces to the right.

He thus realized that the door and the view beyond was a *trompe l'oeil*, the term used for a painting done so skilfully that it fools the eye and looks like an actual scene. And Ruby probably wasn't what she appeared to be either. His guess was that she was a police plant, and never again did he trust a maid. Except, of course, when he was not exercising his profession.

## APHRODITE'S REVENGE

The swatch of cloth was an obvious plant and Zambesi would certainly not manufacture evidence against himself. The chocolate stains were a plant, too, but Cynthia wasn't stupid enough to mention chocolate eclairs if she thought they could connect her with the murder, nor hefty enough to lift and swing a statue which weighed at least fifty pounds. With both Solly and Cynthia in the clear, it follows that Selwyn committed the murder. So much for filial affection.

Selwyn, desperate for more drink money, planned to kill his father. He waited until everybody was asleep before he crept down to the library. After nailing a piece of Solly's jacket to the bottom of the door, Selwyn selected a book and smashed one of the panes of the French door. Then, nibbling on an eclair and hiding behind the door at the right, he waited for Sir Montague to come down and investigate the noise. As soon as Sir Montague's back was turned, Selwyn lifted up the statue and knocked Sir Montague flat. As he fell, his gun went off. Mission accomplished. Selwyn poured himself a stiff drink and went back to bed.

## THE KIDNAPPED KID

Look for a car with a boy; a tall, fat, red-haired blindman; a guide dog, and a driver.

## A MATTER OF GRAVITY

Val killed the doctor. A crack mechanic like Val would not leave a car with a known brake defect at the top of a steep hill. The grass, still bent from a recent disturbance, shows that somebody had recently walked up the path, and only Val had a reason for so doing, as explained below. The greasy hand-marks on the gatepost implicate Val even more.

Dimwiddie reasoned correctly that Val had let the air out of one of the doctor's tyres, had hidden beside the fence, waited until the doctor started to fix the tyre, and then hit him on the back of the head with the jack handle. Val rushed up the hill after throwing the handle away, let his car roll down and either ran down or else, still in the car, jumped out before the crash.

Dimwiddie's first doubts came from the position of the doctor's body although the Speedster hadn't budged. As Dimwiddie put it, mechanics are not equipped to get away with murder.

## THE PERFECT ACE

**Colonel Mustard** was a frustrated man because the town bore was driving away customers. Since few things change in a small village, the Colonel concocted a plan to get rid of the major which depended on everything being the same as it had always been except for one difference.

As owner of the pub, he had ample uninterrupted time to move the metal toestop to the exact angle that would cause One-Eyed Mulligan to hit to the left of the dartboard, and at the exact point where Major Bixby always sat. With the notoriety of the murder, business at The Perfect Ace thrived. The Colonel, however, was not happy. He wished he'd thought of the idea long ago.

## OH MY GOD!

Mrs. Peacock's nephew whose French background was indicated by a beret and a pack of French cigarettes (Gauloises bleu) was a prime suspect. He and his gang planted a bomb and then decided that the bulge in the rug would be a give-away. They therefore masked it by booby trapping the entire room.

## THE POWDER ROOM

Dimwiddie immediately eliminated most of the suspects. He reasoned that Mrs. White was probably too old to have committed the crime, that

Señora Cordoba had a injured arm and that Mademoiselle Fifi's lap dog would probably have barked and brought Mrs. White rushing into the room. Therefore Dame Winifred was the most likely murderess, and he was sure of it after a close look. She had an Adam's Apple, and women don't.

In fact, Dame Winifred turned out to be none other than Gaston Rococco, man of a thousand faces, the notorious contract killer. He took advantage of Felicia's presence and Mrs. White's temporary absence to slip a fast-acting poison into her champagne cocktail, and calmly waited for the poison to take effect. He then carried her lifeless body over to the linen chest, managed to get most of her inside, and draped a towel over her foot just as Mademoiselle Fifi appeared. He was waltzing with Professor Plum when Constable Dimwiddie asked him to come to the powder room for questioning.

## INTO THIN AIR

The Reverend Green needed both hands to hold his camera, and Colonel Mustard was busy lighting his pipe. With everybody occupied and fascinated by the countess, **Professor Plum** had his chance. He'd already arranged for little Rupert to explode his balloons and go into a tantrum, all of which enabled Plum to grab the jewel and thrust it into the confines of the chandelier. In essence, Plum used the magician's technique of diverting attention while performing the basic trick. Thus Plum got a diamond pendant, whereas little Rupert got nothing except some dirty looks on the part of everybody present. But then, as Plum observed, Rupert had to learn that this was an unjust world, and what better teacher than his father?

## INTO THINNER AIR

The bun. The absence of any crumbs proves that the bun was neither cut nor bitten into, and it was obviously easy to lift up the cherry, insert the pendant and then restore the cherry to its former place. And Plum did exactly that.

## THE HARVEST SUPPER

Dimwiddie, enjoying the soup and savouries, saw the stain on the jacket that Mustard had left behind, saw the stains on the table. After considering their relationship, he leaned back and admired both the ingenuity of the scheme, and his own cleverness in solving it.

**Colonel Mustard**, he reasoned, had poisoned his own soup by pouring the poison, probably from a salt shaker. He then managed to claim two seats and gave up one of them as Guy approached. As Guy sat down, Mustard stuck his elbow in Guy's soup and spilled some of it on the table. Mustard, faking embarrassment, was effuse in his apologies and offered to replace Guy's soup with his own, which he had previously poisoned.

A sacrilege, Dimwiddie thought, to poison such good soup, and he wondered whether it had tasted any better with the poison. He shook his head sadly, for that, he would never know.

## FEMME FATALE

**Green.** He was the last to see her, since he complained that his drink was warm, the ice was melted, and that she was drunk. Neither Plum or Mustard mentioned that she'd had too much to drink, and it follows that they saw her in an earlier stage of intoxication.

As related later by Green, the events were as follows: Henrietta tried to sell him some phoney stock, whereupon he called her a liar and a fraud. At this, she flared up and tried to hit him with her Diana. He fended her off without too much trouble, but he pushed too hard, and she fell against the table and fractured her skull.

Afraid that the police would suspect him of foul play, he tried to make it look like suicide. Knowing her reputation for fast living he put the pills and drink around her bath. Then he carefully arranged her in the tub. However, in his panic-stricken state, he poured the cocktail into a brandy glass and scattered pills from an unused bottle. Such a set-up did not impress Dimwiddie who was a stickler for detail.

## MEMORIES OF THE BULL RING

**Plum.** The spacing of the wounds matches the spacing of the pitchfork. Eudocia in screaming at the children, had angered her husband once too often, and after everybody had left, he ran her through with the pitchfork and then wiped off the blood on the tines by piercing them into the turnips. He then resumed his statuesque pose. Dimwiddie, after sizing up the situation, noticed that two turnips had extra holes. Consequently he picked up the turnips one by one and impounded them for the inquest.

## TILL DEATH DO US PART

**Green,** because he is the only one who had both motive and opportunity, and because neither Sindbad nor Fabius found the bust. If they had, they would never have gone off together, with Fabius riding piggyback and with one of them carrying a fifty pound bust of gold, for the possession of which they'd just been fighting.

Apparently they had just broken off the fight with the realization that neither of them had Lady Millicent's bust, when Dimwiddie called out. Faced with a common danger and each afraid that the other would accuse him of attempted grave robbery, they experienced a burst of friendship, and Sindbad hoisted Fabius on his back and escaped with him through the lychgate.

Green did not visit the cemetery, as did the other two, because he knew that the bust was no longer there. He and no one else had the opportunity of taking the bust between the time he'd closed the coffin and had it loaded onto a hearse; anyone else would have had the insurmountable problem of concealing the bust while walking off with it.

Dimwiddie realized this and obtained the warrant to search Green's establishment. There he found not only Lady Millicent's bust, but an unusually fine collection of jewellery which Green had thoughtfully removed from various caskets before burying them. Accused, Green said, "What harm, when not a single one ever objected?" Dimwiddie was not convinced.

## MAKING TRACKS

Professor Plum finally lit the hot air balloon with one of his many sheets of calculations. Before he was asked to, Reverend Green started to throw out the weighty religious tomes which were to act as ballast. Professor Plum dropped the map of Algeria as the balloon shot away. Were they too old to join the foreign legion anyway he wondered? Reverend Green accidentally threw out their ballooning manual, *The Ascent of Man.*

Mrs. White dropped a bottle of her secret sauce from the front basket of her motorized bicycle. The trailing balloon anchor caught up a hoop and swept her cook's hat from her head. She swerved dropping her carefully-packed fish kettle (no cook is ever parted from her secret sauce or her fish kettle). She'd now have to rely on improvisation if she was going to make it in China.

Colonel Mustard shaved off his moustache in the fountain and changed into his tennis shoes. He had had a flat and smoked three pipes whilst changing the wheel. He wiped his oily hands on his handkerchief and raced down the drive on his way to Monte Carlo crushing his press in his haste.

Mrs. Peacock broke her turquoise beads while lowering the trolley and yelled at Miss Scarlet who was making another final adjustment to her cupid's bow. "You can go in the back", she shouted, dashing the mirror to the ground. "Whose bright idea was this", she muttered as they unloaded the pantomime horse off the trolley, climbed in and trotted off not noticing that one of its spots had fallen off. "I certainly hope Jake Jasper hasn't gotten too far", Miss Scarlet sighed.